REDEEMING MEG

BLACK SWAN DIVISION, BOOK 1

MISTY EVANS
NOLAN EVANS

Beach
Path
Publishing

There are some things you learn best in calm, and some in storm. ~Willa Cather, The Song of the Lark

BLACK SWAN DEFINITION

A black swan is an unpredictable event beyond what is typically expected of a situation and has potentially severe consequences.

Black swan events are characterized by their extreme rarity, severe impact, and the widespread insistence they were obvious in hindsight.

Unmask the Shadows. Face the Truth. Survive the Impossible.

The *Black Swan Division* thriller series is a pulse-pounding blend of high-stakes espionage, gritty action, and unforgettable characters.

When the world's most volatile threats demand a response beyond the reach of conventional forces, the Black Swan Division answers the call.

Led by fearless undercover operative Meg Carson

and her enigmatic second-in-command Declan Reid, this elite CIA team specializes in missions no one else can handle—missions where failure isn't an option.

From international conspiracies to rogue assassins, the team navigates deadly terrains, all while wrestling with fractured loyalties, personal demons, and secrets that could destroy them from within.

The *Black Swan Division* series delivers heart-stopping twists, nonstop action, and a dash of slow-burn romance. Each book draws you deeper into a web of deception, daring escapes, and the kind of heroism that tests the limits of trust and courage.

Join the mission. The Black Swan Division is waiting.

ONE

Platja Fonda, Spain

IT WASN'T every day you had to face all your demons at once. Today was Meg Carson's day.

The lazy afternoon sun turned the sea into a carpet of diamonds, small boats bobbing in the clear blue waters. It was the off-season, and tourists were scarce, yet a smattering of local children ran among the waves. Their mothers gathered in groups on blankets, watching and gossiping along the rocky shoreline.

Nestled at the foot of the high cliffs, Meg still felt vulnerable, even with a wall of rock shielding her and the others from town. Shielding her, she hoped, from life.

Warm, humid air tickled her nose. Her skin gleamed with sweat. The towel under her was already soaked through. Rare for this late in the season, but the week had seen multiple days with temps above average. Seemed everywhere she went, she brought the unexpected and unusual.

The rocking of the boats eased her overtaxed mind into a lull. Here, she could forget everything. Be no one. Decide what was next.

A wave hit an outcropping of large stones to the north, white spray climbing high in the air before dropping once more into the hidden cove. She admired those rocks, taking the constant battering of the sea without crumbling. Impenetrable, unyielding. If only she could make her heart so solid and resistant.

Footsteps approached from behind her. Snapping out of the lull of the sea, her focus shifted. Even in the mineral-laden sand, she could hear how purposeful the steps were. Sense the person was on a mission, and that mission involved her. Instinct and finely honed skills made her slip a hand under the towel.

The cool metal of her Bodyguard 380 instantly mollified her. The scent of her sister's signature floral perfume did, too.

A shadow fell over her, and Meg returned her hand to the lounge chair's arm, pasting on a fake smile. "Kids napping?"

Tawny and Josh had invited Meg to accompany them and her niece and nephew on this vacation. Meg needed a vacation from her life, but beggars couldn't be choosers.

Tawny, hair in a high ponytail and concern etched in her features, held out Meg's cell. The screen showed a live call on mute. "Your boss."

"I don't have—" *a boss anymore.* Yet, a shiver of anticipation snaked through her. She knew exactly who was on the line, and while Tawny had no idea her older sister had been an elite covert operative for six years, there was a part of Meg who both hated and missed that life. "I'm retired. It's a telemarketer or a wrong number. Hang up."

Dangerous, that, but Meg had told him—told them all —never to bother her again. To go to hell and stay there. She was done. Period. End of story.

Tawny crouched next to the chair, her eyes wide with fear. "I already tried that. He's called three times. He says if I don't get you on the line, he'll tell Josh about..." She squeezed her eyes shut and dropped her voice to a whisper. "About what happened." Those hazel eyes, so much like their mother's, opened once more. "Meg, how does your boss know about that weekend?"

The best spy in the business, now CIA's Director of Operations. He knew or could find out anything. Leverage, blackmail, manipulation. He was a master at them all.

Meg hated Conrad Flynn for that. Hated him for scaring her sister. "He's bluffing, and besides, Josh would never hold it against you. He adores you, and you have a great life with him." *One I intend to see continues.* "You should tell him yourself and clear the air. It was a meaningless flirtation before you were married."

Tawny took Meg's hand and force-wrapped her fingers around the phone. "Talk to this guy. Please. For me." Her eyes added, *and for you.* Desperation clouded Tawny's face. "You're miserable, Meg, even in this paradise with people who love you. Maybe you should think about going back. Jessie would want that."

Meg considered whipping the phone into the waves. Just hearing that name made her want to scream. The grief and guilt balled up inside her threatened to explode. Tawny believed Jessica Mendoza had been an employee of her security firm—a cover they'd used for their special division of spies.

Instead of losing control, Meg did what she always did these days—she bitch-slapped the scream down into the deepest crater inside her. Pasting on the fake smile again, she hugged her sister. "I'll handle it. Go kiss your husband and tell him you love him. Everything will be alright. I promise."

Tawny hugged her back, then trudged away. "I love you, Meggie," she called over her shoulder, her voice carrying on the breeze.

Staring at the phone, Meg forced her erratic pulse to slow. It was a phone conversation. Not a commitment.

She unmuted the call and lifted the device to her ear. "If you ever threaten my sister again, I'll shove your balls in a blender."

"Good to hear your voice, too," Conrad Flynn replied. "It's been a while. Enjoying Spain? By the way, you'll have to get in line for that honor."

"Whatever it is you want, no." She disconnected.

As expected, the phone rang almost immediately. She counted to ten, willing it to go to voicemail, then remembered the scared look on her sister's face and jabbed the button. "What?"

"We've got a missing friend in Bucharest. The president has reactivated your division."

Black Swan. A whopping four people, the elite of the elite in what had been dubbed Flynn's Secret Army. Two men, two women, who could work in pairs or alone. Get in, get out, complete the mission without anyone ever knowing.

Only now, one was dead and the division was, too. "I quit, remember?" The MIA had to be someone important for the president to get involved. "Find another sucker to track down your MIA."

"He requested you, and you're not on search and rescue. At least, not for our friend. Your mission is more critical."

Meg's pulse stuttered. "What is it?"

"Special circumstances that can't be discussed over an open line, but you might turn on the news. The Bucharest embassy is under attack, and we have a black swan. Mosai Hagar is involved. Thousands of innocent people could be harmed."

Her mouth went dry. Her group had been formed to handle what their name suggested—an unpredictable event with potentially severe consequences. Such events were characterized by their extreme rarity, severe impact, and the widespread insistence they were obvious in hindsight. Nine-eleven was considered a black swan, but such events were never obvious, even in hindsight.

Since then, such occurrences had been increasing. The world grew ever more chaotic. No matter how much the analysts tried to predict situations and outcomes, the outliers and challenges grew unhindered, thus the need for a team that could move quickly, quietly, and counter whatever was taking place.

"Playing the innocent card is a low blow, and you have others who can protect them."

Flynn agreed. "You'll want in on this when you find out who the MIA is, trust me."

"Not..." *Declan.* She couldn't even say his name. "My...second?"

Dec Reid had been her right-hand man in more ways than Flynn or anyone else outside her team knew. "Not that bastard—hell, if it was him, I wouldn't even be worried. He'd fight his way out, no matter what. I can't give you anything else at this point. You're going to have to have faith. You will want to be in on this."

Faith. Trust. Did she even know what those terms meant anymore? "I can't."

Once again, she hung up.

In his time in the field, Conrad Flynn hadn't just climbed through Dante's nine circles of hell, he'd created them. He'd even gone under the deepest cover possible— faking his own death—to root out a mole in the CIA. Since coming in from the cold and being reinstated by the Agency—and receiving more commendations than she could count—he'd surprisingly thrived behind a desk. Not that he always stayed there.

Her phone rang again. She ground her teeth and punched the button. "You are a dog on a bone, you know that?"

"There's a key under the plant in your bedroom that

goes to a locker in the Bucharest train station." Flynn was done with small talk. "You'll find a survival kit waiting. I'm sending the rest of the swans to assist. I know I gave you my word I'd leave you alone, but I have to break that promise, and yes, you can kill me later. Right now, I need you to get off that pink lounge chair and get yourself to Romania. You've been reactivated, Meg."

Click. The line went dead.

Tit for tat.

Bastard.

...get off that pink lounge chair...

Her eyes slid to the left, then right. Was he here?

Doubtful, but he loved nothing better than to jump into an op himself, and someone had to be tailing her. Either that or Flynn's favorite techie, Del, had a satellite pointed at this very beach so her ex-boss could harass her while he sent someone to sneak a key into her room at the villa.

Not beyond reason. She held up her middle finger and waved it around, hoping he was across the ocean watching from his cushy leather office chair inside Langley.

I'm sending the rest of the swans...

She should call him back and tell him, "Hard pass." How could she face them? The other swans...

Wait, what am I thinking? How could she even consider complying, with or without the rest of her team?

For a long moment, her focus returned to watching the boats bob on the water. Listening to the kids' delighted cries as they played. She couldn't go back to the

CIA. Wouldn't. Being the leader of her team had been the best—and worst—experience of her life, but her heart couldn't take it. Losing a friend was terrible, but Jessie's death had been...

A horror Meg wouldn't wish on her worst enemy.

The look on her friend's bruised and bloody face right before Mosai Hagar swung the machete hadn't been accusing. There'd been no fear or judgment. As the man holding Meg had sunk his hand in her hair and forced her to watch, Jessie had stared at her with sad but trusting eyes. "It's okay," she'd whispered through her cracked, swollen lips. "You couldn't save—"

Me. The word was lost forever on a swing of that damn machete. Jessie would never speak again.

Meg blinked hard against the onslaught of tears. If she let even one slip out, the dam would break.

She stood and slowly walked to the edge of the lapping water. One of the kids waved at her.

Hagar is involved.

How many innocents would he harm? Why attack the embassy? Who was the missing person?

Tommy. Her heart lurched as his thin face and big eyes flashed through her memory. It couldn't be. He was safe in the US.

Wasn't he?

Jessie had gotten him a job with the Agency as an analyst. He'd put in for an overseas position. They'd sent him to Afghanistan during the pullout, and two hours after he'd landed, his sister had been murdered.

My fault.

Meg toyed with the phone, aching to call Flynn and make sure Jessie's brother was okay. Instead, she dialed Tommy's number.

The call went to voicemail. A generic, computerized bot instructed her to leave a message, except the mailbox was full. Tommy never used a voice assistant—the nerd loved to personalize his recordings with random Neitchze quotes. His favorite? *He who has a why to live can bear almost any how.*

Puzzles and mysteries always sucked Meg in. Getting revenge did, too.

She waved back at the young boy. He motioned for her to join him and his friends. "Do you want to play?" he called in Spanish.

I have to speak for her. Make sure Tommy's not involved with this. It would be just like him to go after Hagar alone. "Not today," she replied.

Then she reared back and, with all her might, chucked the phone into the sea. There was a key waiting for her and her own personal why.

TWO

DECLAN REID WAS three days past needing a shower, six months past a haircut.

Surrounded by crates of military cargo and the mindless drone of four C-5M Super Galaxy engines miles over the ocean, his mind was elsewhere. Only hours before, he'd been trading bullets with a Colombian cartel on the outskirts of Bogotá. Now, he had bigger problems.

Much bigger.

Meg.

Declan took a deep breath and shoved the thought away. He was a professional. One woman wasn't going to commandeer ten years of intense training.

The cavernous interior of the C-5 cargo plane was dimly lit with the ghostly glow of LED lighting strips silhouetting rows of giant cargo crates packed tightly together. The air was stale and cold. The behemoth of a plane was never meant to transport people. There was barely enough room for stretching, less matter standing. It was enough to make anyone claustrophobic.

It didn't seem to bother Spencer Sterling.

"You're going to get us killed one of these days," Declan called out.

Spence and Declan had been in more tight spots together than he could count, but being smuggled onto a military supply run as crates of 'tactical equipment' was a new one for both of them. Five hours in the cargo bay with nothing but their thoughts had put them both on edge. Or so he had thought. Spence actually seemed to be enjoying himself.

The bastard chuckled. Moving nimbly from stack to stack, exploring the containers in the bay, a resounding thud echoed each time he jumped between gaps in the stacks.

Who knew what was in those crates?

"Any word from Del?" He maneuvered back to where Declan sat. Del was their eyes and ears and had more technical expertise in computer systems than anyone at Langley. If he couldn't get through to them on the Galaxy, no one could.

"Nothing yet." Declan touched his earpiece, making sure it was still functioning.

The pair had been assisting the local drug enforcement agency in Bogotá with a group of cartels that had put a US Ambassador at risk. After cornering a few members of the gang on the west side of the city, a tense standoff situation had ended with Flynn—the man himself—on a phone call telling the duo they were being pulled out. Flynn rarely spoke directly to operatives. That alone spoke to the urgency and importance of the new mission. Team Pegasus had arrived shortly after, and despite his questions, Declan had followed orders.

Trusting your team kept you alive.

All Flynn had said was that he had a crucial mission that he knew they would *want* to be part of. That's what had caused a cascade of questions in Declan's mind. Flynn refused to tell them more over a public line. *Get to the C47 Mil base. Your ride is waiting. Del will contact you. Meg Carson will be awaiting your arrival in Romania.*

The last statement echoed in Declan's head.

Shit. The Swans had been reactivated.

He'd hoped they might one day but had never imagined Megan Carsen would be part of them again. Their leader.

Turbulence rocked the plane, sending Spence stumbling and snapping Declan back to the present. He instantly touched the familiar grip of his Sig Sauer P320 as his other hand smacked one of the crates to steady him. *Just turbulence.*

Spence took a seat next to him on a metal bench crowded with black plastic containers that had been tied down. "Jesus, Dec, I haven't seen you this worked up in a while."

Spence didn't know yet that Meg would be waiting for them. "I'm fine. Just want to know what's going on."

Declan was in his element when he had the big picture. Never one to rush into a situation, he always considered all of the options available to him and his team.

Six years in the Marines, a spec ops stint, and ending up on an Anti-Terrorism Security Team had put him on the CIA's radar. When an op went sideways in Syria, and he'd been lucky to see another sunrise, he'd assumed he was done. Finished. *Put a bullet in my head*-kind of cooked with his career.

Conrad Flynn had had another idea.

Static blared in his ears. Del.

"Black Swan Two, this is Loch Ness. Come in. Over."

And...here we go. "This is Swan Two," Declan responded. "Never thought I'd hear that callout over comms again. Over."

Del was silent for a pregnant breath. "Neither did I, but our current situation calls for it. We've got a highly-sensitive red bag retrieval mission, and we need a team that isn't on record... anywhere. We need our best gents... and ladies."

Dec and Spence locked eyes briefly. This was going to be bad.

Del continued. "Mosai Hagar and his death squad have made major progress on recruiting recently, and they're looking stronger and more organized than we've ever seen. Bin Laden type-power. Only they're not staying in the shadows. They're striking where it counts and obtaining top-secret information that may lead to a lot of people getting hurt. They're currently after a thumb drive in the Bucharest US Embassy. They've already incited a considerable local uprising, and we believe they'll use those folks to overwhelm security. He's not on the scene yet, but we anticipate his arrival. We can't let the intel on that drive fall into his hands."

"Stopping an uprising isn't under our umbrella," Declan said. "Are we after the drive, or are we taking out Hagar?"

"The drive is your target. It's inside a safe in the chief of mission's office. There's also a more personal interest—Tommy Mendoza. He's missing. We need him back."

Tommy. Declan hadn't thought about the kid since they'd all attended Jessie's funeral. Tommy had sent a roundhouse punch into Dec's face.

Granted, it was deserved, but...

I can never make it right.

"What the hell is he doing in Bucharest?"

"His job. He's been there for eight months."

Right. An analyst who'd lost his shit after his sister's murder was broadcast on social media was now working at the embassy? What was he really there for? "What's he got to do with the red bag?"

"We believe he's the one who discovered the intel the drive contains. His superior didn't realize how important it was. Until Tommy disappeared."

Idiot.

"Kidnapped?" Spence asked.

"Status unknown," Del replied, giving them no hint. Tommy might be dead for all anyone knew.

Dead. Declan rubbed his eyes. Meg wasn't ready for this.

Hell, *he* wasn't ready for this.

"The Black Swan Division was put out to pasture for a reason, Loch Ness. Why does Solomon want to resurrect us?" Solomon was Flynn's call name—the former codename he'd used while undercover in the field.

"More importantly," Spence added, "if Declan is still Swanny Two, does that mean I'm Swanny One now?"

He never could be serious.

Del's exasperated sigh could be heard in Russia. "Above my pay grade, Two. I'm here to keep you guys alive and moving. And no, Three, your status hasn't changed. You're meeting Swan One in Bucharest. She's en route as we speak. She'll be lead on the mission, just like always."

Lead? Spence seemed to echo Declan's shock, his brows hitting his hairline. *They're bringing Meg back?* he mouthed.

Declan nodded. Spence used his hands to simulate the top of his head exploding.

Right there with you, buddy.

Del continued, "You have a limited window before the embassy goes tits ups, and you're back on US soil. Twelve hours from the meet-up. That's it, gentlemen. Retrieve the drive, locate Tommy if possible, and meet Pegasus for extraction at the rendezvous point. Coordinates will be sent closer to extraction time. Don't be late. You will be left behind."

"Easy for you to say," Declan grumbled under his breath. That cushy chair in Langley had never seen Del be late in his life, but then Del had a reserved parking space and plenty of amenities to make his job a cakewalk compared to theirs. He spoke louder this time, emphasizing his words. "Is Swan One stable?"

The hum of the engines made Del's hesitation even more obvious. Spence shifted uncomfortably where he stood, avoiding Declan's eyes this time.

Finally, Del responded. "If you have questions, I can put Solomon on the line."

Del said it almost as if it were a threat. *Which meant what?* Declan bit down on his tongue to stop his flippant reply. Like hell, Flynn would discuss Meg's mental status with them. They were about to be in the trenches together against Hagar and his death squad. Of course, he would say she was capable. Stable.

But is she? Or was Flynn up shit creek and had no one left to turn to? Declan's pulse raced beneath his skin. Probably the latter.

"Beggars can't be choosers, eh?" Spence quipped.

Del didn't acknowledge him. "You'll be running dark once we terminate this connection until you're reunited with the rest of your team."

The rest of the team equaled one member—Meg.

"If things go sideways, what's our contingency plan?" Spence asked, no joking now.

"Just like old times. You're on your own."

Declan sighed. It was probably better that way. Outside contact usually had a way of making things messy. But this felt wrong. Off. Not unusual for Black Swan missions, but still. This was off like the leaning Tower of Pisa-off.

Training and experience had a funny way of honing one's sixth sense. His gut never lied.

Del's voice squawked over the earpiece. "Any last questions?"

He had plenty. "You saw her last eval. Give it to me straight. Is she going to be a problem?" Declan needed Meg in top form. If she was off the deep end, she could put them all at risk, intentionally or not.

"Any *other* questions?" Del's voice had an audible eye roll in it.

"Yes, but you won't answer them," Declan growled in frustration. *Maybe Flynn should get on the line.*

"Look...those evals are classified. I haven't seen them."

Bullshit. Del could access anything he wanted, classified or not. He was the best of the best. There was a reason Flynn used him. "Like hell, you haven't."

Del paused again. His voice came out lower. Declan could barely him over the plane noise. "She's Orange, but passed every one of her last tests."

Fucking. Hell. The color labels were a classification system Flynn used for evaluating competency in the field. Regardless of what tests he'd put her through, she was orange...

She shouldn't even be allowed out of Langley. *Fucking Flynn. Fucking Black Swan Division. Fuck.*

"As I recall, she quit. How did Solomon get her back?"

Del's tone returned to business, ignoring the question. "Good luck, swans. Radio contact will resume at twelve hundred hours local time. Loch Ness out."

Outwardly, he remained stone cold, but inside, Declan raged. Every piece of this mission was its own bullet, just waiting to fire and cause irreparable damage.

Meg has to keep it together. If she wasn't thinking clearly, who knew what poor decisions she would make?

And more than anything, she would have something to prove to herself. Despite having clean hands, Meg blamed herself for Jessie's death.

Blamed him, too.

What a shit show.

The swans had once been the elite of the elite. Now? They were their own worst enemy.

And once more, they were going up against Mosai Hagar and his infamous death squad.

THREE

"AUDIO CHECK." Meg adjusted her earpiece and mic. "Testing one-two-three."

"Coming in loud and sort of clear, Black Swan One," Del responded, his voice both reassuring and annoying in her ear. She'd hoped never to hear it again, but sinners in hell wanted ice water, too. "I'm picking up background noise. Can you confirm? Over."

Mother Nature was dumping a monsoon on the city. Even the best technology couldn't eliminate the din of the lashing rain and wind as Meg stood on the sidewalk in front of the towering concrete and glass building in front of her.

At least the storm had drenched the uprising at the embassy and sent all but the truly hardcore protestors scurrying. They'd be back as soon as the fast-moving deluge was over, and that meant Meg had to hurry, downpour or not.

"Confirmed, storm in the area. Visual check." She squeezed her eyes tight, activating the contacts from the 'survival kit' before opening them again. Eagle Eyes, as they were called, not only sharpened her vision but allowed Langley to see what she focused on. She pointedly looked at the Biblioteca Nationala's sign ten floors above her. "Can you read?"

Rain hit her in the face, and she blinked. She was soaked, cold, and hungry. With any luck, she could get in and out of the embassy before Declan and Spence touched down.

Flynn would kill her for going in alone, but he would also praise her if she managed to get the red bag. It wasn't necessarily the color red, it was simply a designation of utmost importance and the highest in classified intel.

A gruff voice superseded Del's. "Why the hell am I looking at the library, Swan One?"

Flynn. He hated it when she went off script. Well, she had a few questions for him, too. "Why don't you have one of the trapped State Department kids bring you the drive?"

"I trust no one but you. I repeat, why are you not at the appointed site?"

While initially gaining Flynn's trust hadn't been easy, it was no compliment that he was now putting the mission's success in her hands. Regardless that the president had reactivated the division, bottom line, he believed she was his best resource to get the job done. Or perhaps, the most expendable one. "I'll stroll through the protestors right up to the front gate and demand they let me enter. I'm sure that will work." She snorted, the sound lost in the downpour. "Besides, getting in is one thing; getting out securely with the package is another."

"Which is why your team will be assisting." The irritation in his voice made her smile. "Get your ass to the embassy."

Thanks to budget cuts and an ongoing war between the House and Senate, the place had been short-staffed. Most activities had been put on hold until funding was appropriated again, making the place ripe for an invasion.

Eastern Europe was already on edge over the Russian chess game going on with the Ukrainians, and plenty of militants and fascists were happy to rile folks up. Even the US Marine Security Guardsmen and Diplomatic Security Service had been caught off guard. They, too, were understaffed at the moment, thanks to tensions in more volatile areas.

"If you trust me, let me do my job." What she needed was an in, an asset who knew the language, the culture, the people. The Poliția Română had been called in to assist with controlling the crowd, but watching the news, she'd seen little to indicate any of them cared. Half of them were probably in Mosai Hagar's pockets. "Over and out."

Jogging across the expanse to the giant entry doors, she muted her mic. She would allow them to see who she was recruiting but not let them hear what needed to be said.

Inside, her shoes squeaked on the marble floor and the sound echoed up, up, up to the ceiling high overhead as she made her way to the escalators. The spirited rain lashed at the tall windows, but the hush in here was deep and comforting, as if this was the calm center of the storm.

As she rode the escalator, she spotted a lone figure at a desk on the second-floor veranda. He paid no attention to her, and she pretended to ignore him while logging his height, weight, and potential weapons.

Old habits died hard.

Her target was shelving a few volumes in a designated area containing a collection of materials on topics covering US culture and lifestyle. The American Corners program had been instituted as a partnership program between the US Embassy and the library, to provide information, programs, and exhibits to further positive relations.

Contessa Vulpe, known as The Architect to those in Flynn's Army, had adopted the look of a nondescript librarian—her rich brown hair was pulled into a tidy bun, oversized glasses sat on her nose, a simple pleated skirt disguised her generous hips—but as her name suggested, she was both a countess and a fox. The former label she'd done her damnedest to escape, but the latter she embraced wholeheartedly. She spoke without turning, her hearing as sharp as ever. "May I help you?" She repeated the question in Romanian, her accent—a good one—thicker as her tongue flowed over the words.

Meg brushed a wet strand from her cheek. "I hope so."

Tessa's hand stilled in mid-air, the book suspended for a heartbeat before she finished sliding it between two other volumes. She didn't turn but lowered her voice to a low growl. "What are *you* doing here? I told you I never wanted to see you again."

Taking a step closer, Meg surveyed the area. Discreet cameras blended into the corners of the large expanse, and probably more were hidden in the overhead lights. There was no reason to bug the library, however. "I need your expertise. I wouldn't ask if it weren't critical to saving a life."

"I can't help you." Continuing to avoid her eyes, Tessa turned to her cart and pushed it down the row. "I don't do that anymore. We're about to close. You should leave."

"Tommy's missing. Could be a kidnapping, or could be he's..." Dead. She couldn't bring herself to say it.

This brought Tessa's attention, finally, to Meg. "I'm sorry to hear that. What does that have to do with me?"

Good thing she couldn't hear Flynn over the earpiece. At the sight of Tessa, Meg imagined he was having a coronary. "I need to get into the embassy. Tonight."

Never taking her focus from Meg, she positioned the cart between them, removing a book from the lower shelf.

She held it to her chest. "That isn't an answer. How did you find me?"

Meg had no doubt there was a small but accurate pistol hidden in the book. "I keep an eye on my enemies."

Her lips twitched. "And your friends?"

A low blow. Meg fought not to break eye contact and reveal her soft spot. "I'm not here to discuss what happened to Jessie. I need to get into the embassy undetected. We can do this the easy way or the hard way."

Tessa snorted. "Perhaps if you and your government paid more attention to your so-called friends, the chaos at the embassy wouldn't have happened." Placing the book in reach, she chose another from the cart and examined it. "Why can't you walk in the front door?"

Another dig, and it probably had layers of meaning, but Meg didn't have time to dissect them, nor did she care. "It's your government, too, and I know they had you design a backdoor into the place when it was built. Service tunnels, secret entrances, hidden passageways. Show me the plans, and I'll be out of your hair."

"You think I keep such things here? What, I have them tattooed on my ass?" Her dark brown eyes flashed from behind the thick lenses of her glasses. "Go to hell and take whoever sent you. Get out of my library."

"No one sent me. This is all me. Hagar is watching. He's the one stirring this up. You're my only hope to get in and out without him knowing." She didn't want to divulge everything, but... "I suspect Tommy stumbled over something damning, and Hagar knows it. That intel is buried inside the embassy. My mission is to retrieve it."

"Easy job. You don't need me." But her eyes told a different story. The fox was curious. She loved a challenge. More so if she would outwit a terrorist with her skills. "Even if I could help, why would I? You let her die."

Bad blood ran deep. Too many years ago, Jessie had been Tessa's star pupil at The Farm when Meg and Jessie were in training. Tactical stealth entries and exits had been taken to an entirely new level with the fox. "Her death is on me. I've never claimed otherwise, and you have no reason to believe I have your back, but it's *not* an easy job, and you know it. I can't trust anyone else."

A thin eyebrow rose. The fox wanted more, and although she'd never admit it, she, herself, had a backdoor —her heart.

Give her a reason to take the bait. "I'm only doing this for Jessie," Meg admitted. That much was true. "And Tommy. I can't ever make it right, but I can make Hagar pay. My team will assist, but I have to watch their backs as well. It's all on me. I need to get in and out as quickly as possible."

Endless seconds passed. Tessa returned to shelving, purposely making Meg sweat. "No," she finally said. "I won't help you."

Damn. Meg buried her frustrated sigh. She'd known it was a long shot. "I understand." Truth was, she did. She wished she'd stuck to her guns with Flynn. "I'm sorry I bothered you. Have a good life working in this Romanian library, where your skills and talents are going to waste."

With that, she turned, a brief feeling of satisfaction at Tessa's gasp making her lips quirk. *I'll figure it out. I'll find another way.*

"I said I won't help *you*," Tessa called. "I never said I wouldn't help Declan and Spencer."

Meg pinched her lips together, keeping the triumphant grin off her face as she stopped and faced the woman. Declan was good for something, after all. "They'll meet us."

Tessa shoved the cart away, grabbing the book with the gun. She reached for the back of her bun, and her hair cascaded over her shoulders. She removed the glasses and headed for the escalator. "Let's go then. They need me."

FOUR

Midnight

   Service tunnels under Bucharest

"COME TO BUCHAREST, THEY SAID." Spence raised a boot out of the muck and made a face. "We'll get together, have a few laughs."

Declan squeezed his flashlight. The beam bounced off the sides of the underground tunnel. "If you're going to quote my favorite movie, don't screw up the lines."

The skinny boy leading the way through the maze turned a grinning face on them. He couldn't be more than ten or twelve. "Die Hard, *mda*? Great film." His dirty hands flew through the air, mimicking a karate chop before he pointed at himself. "Van Damme, my favorite."

Why the fuck had Meg set this up as their meeting place? The tunnel was only about a hundred feet below the streets above, and much of the city's waste, water, and sewage ended up there one way or another. The stench was nearly unbearable, and there was a more sinister smell lingering underneath. Death.

Their boots echoed on wet stone as they trudged along the dimly lit corridors. The faint screeching and chirping of rats lingered around corners and clung to the shadows. How did anything survive down here?

Despite the conditions, gangs of orphaned and runaway children frequented the tunnels. Much like the malnourished kid ahead of them, most were homeless and relied on each other for food and protection.

The place felt like an Orson Scott Card novel. Despite being eight, ten, twelve years old at the most, these kids lived and fought like adults. They were tough. He would think twice about turning his back on one.

"How long have you lived down here, Van Damme?" Spence asked the kid.

The boy brightened at the nickname. "Forever. Bruce Lee, he takes care of us."

Sure he did. The stench overpowered Declan's nose again. As horrible as it was, he'd smelled worse. Seen it, too. Thousands packed under a bridge in Afghanistan, moaning from hunger pains and withdrawal from opioids. Hundreds rounded up and slaughtered in pits in Siberia.

The list went on. Most of it didn't affect him anymore. At least, that's what he told himself, anyway. He couldn't afford to let it.

Nightmares and flashbacks weren't the half of it. He

swore the ghosts of those he hadn't saved tried to suffo-
cate him every damn night.

Deeper and deeper they went. People were piled
together in spots. Could they avoid this Bruce Lee char-
acter who controlled the tunnels?

A man like any other, but one who had set himself up
as king, he could be trouble for them. He could stop them
from getting to their destination. He might even kill
them.

Declan was no psychologist, but he understood men
like Bruce Lee well. Their motivations were often illogical, and their reactions and decisions were based on the
moment, not any long-term plan or wisdom gained
through life experience. They lived in the moment, never
knowing if they would make it to the next day, month, or
year.

Yet, the system this man had set up showed he had
the smarts to take advantage of his own people while
providing a strange form of protection and oddball family
for them.

Strangers, however, we're a double-edged sword.
They might provide food, money, and other favors, yet at
the same time, be seen as a threat. Their team needed to
present as an ally, not an enemy.

Declan had already promised their young guide a
hundred Romanian leu. Cheap by most standards but
approximately equal to a hundred US dollars. A sum that
would make the Van Damme fan rich.

That said, the kid had wanted Declan's boots to sell
to one of his tunnel mates for a better spot to sleep, closer

to the heat pipes. No deal—not only did Declan need the damn things, they were his lucky tact pair. They'd climbed mountains, slogged through bogs, roamed desserts, and kicked plenty of lowlife ass through the years. He didn't understand why they hadn't fallen apart yet, but like him, maybe they were too damn stubborn.

To appease the boy, Declan had dangled the carrot of his pocket knife that contained fourteen different tools. The kid's eyes kept sliding to the pocket where Declan had stuffed it away. For him and many of his friends, tangible goods—tools, boots, weapons—were more valuable than money.

Not much fit that category for him. A few people, including the one he was walking with and the one he was about to meet. Too bad Meg hated him.

The commendations in his CIA folder made him look like a hero—a loyal, experienced, and elite soldier for his country. At one time, that was enough. Up until the day he'd met Meg Ann Carson.

His whole life changed after that.

He'd ordered himself not to fall in love with her. Had done it anyway. He'd demanded his heart not go belly up like a trained dog every time she walked into a room. He'd failed that, as well.

Over and over again, he'd fallen for her. Let her manipulate his feelings for her in a way no one else had ever done.

And then she'd sucked him into The Black Swans to use his skills and competency to balance her brilliant mind. He'd been her biggest supporter and her fiercest devil's advocate—exactly what she'd wanted him to do as her second in command. Challenge her, test her, back her up when shit hit the fan.

She hated failure as much as he did, and it had been the two of them together who could take any challenge and look at it from all angles. Their team could provide the outcome needed for any goatfuck, no matter what sacrifice had to be made.

Until that sacrifice had been one of their own.

Jessie's face tormented him every time he closed his eyes. That brutal swing of the machete. The sound when it connected.

His nightmares were filled with that sound. With Meg's screams.

His waking moments with the ring of her hateful accusations.

Her hate, period.

For what he'd done.

For what he *hadn't* done.

Saved Meg at the expense of Jessie. Saved the woman he loved by sacrificing one of the teammates they'd both sworn to protect.

He and Spence rounded another corner. People of all ages huddled together for warmth. Their pale, thin, and dirty bodies were unnaturally still. Many didn't even appear to be breathing.

Some days—hell, most of them—he wished he wasn't. That he could go back in time and offer himself in exchange for Jessie. Meg would still hate him if he were dead, but maybe she'd still love him, too.

The tunnel narrowed to an entrance with metal bars. The kid began outlining his favorite Van Damme film, complete with more punches, kicks, and quotes from his hero. With his lithe body, he slipped through the bars easily, but Declan and Spence had to remove their jackets and holstered guns to squeeze between them.

Even then, Declan had to suck in his breath as hard as he could to pass his muscled upper body through the tight space. It was touch and go, Spence egging him on when he got stuck. He had to stretch his arms overhead, sucking in his stomach but keeping his ribs from flaring in order to become like one of the bars himself.

Spence and the kid both tugged on him from the other side, the kid grabbing his thigh while Spence grabbed his belt. "One, two, three," Spence said.

Declan sucked in another deep breath and imagined himself being as skinny as the two of them. They yanked and tugged, and it hurt like hell, but finally, he broke through to the other side. Off balance, he tumbled to the slippery, wet stones, his knee barking when it hit hard.

He heaved a couple of deep breaths before getting to his feet. He'd probably have bruised ribs tomorrow.

"Put on a few pounds, have you?" Spence joked.

He accepted his coat and weapon from him. "I'm at fighting weight, just like always."

"Sure you are, mate."

"Van Damme always lean," the kid told him. "You should be more like him."

Slipping on the holster before donning the jacket, he cocked his chin at the kid to get going. A set of iron steps led to a utility tunnel with pumps, pipes as big around as a man, and intricate groupings of valves.

As they cleared the top, his breath whooshed out at the sight of who awaited them.

He'd known he would see her after nearly a year of forcing himself not to interfere in her retirement. Had prepped himself for this very moment when they'd come face to face again.

What a joke.

Nothing could prepare him for seeing her up and close and personal, even after all this time.

She was thinner, her hair longer. She'd pulled the lush blond strands back in a ponytail, emphasizing her cheekbones and heart-shaped chin. Her eyes, always serious, had that haunted look that made him want to drop to his knees.

He wasn't the only one tortured by Jessie's death. Meg had always been wary and on guard, but after that night, the tormented, anguished expression had never left her.

Even now, after she'd been formally cleared of any wrongdoing, had gone through months of therapy, and had jetted off to exotic locals to rest and recoup, she looked as anguished as he felt.

Spence charged forward, lifting her off the ground. "There you are." He hugged her hard, Meg stiffening in his embrace. Spence didn't seem to care. He set her back but didn't loosen his hold on her as he scanned her from head to toe. "Gods, you look good. All tan and such. What beach have you been gracing, sunshine?"

She pulled away, giving him a faint smile. "Good to see you, too."

Contessa Vulpe was with her.

Interesting.

"Tess." Spence offered a hand to The Architect. "It's been a minute, eh, luv?"

"Get over here, you," she said, throwing her arms around his neck. Then she turned to Declan. "Quit frowning, Dec. You look constipated."

He allowed her to embrace him while all his senses stayed tuned to Meg. Had she recruited Tessa for this mission? "Imagine meeting you here."

"I know." She stepped back, a cunning grin on her face. "Strange bedfellows and all that, right?"

"Enough chatter," Meg said. "We need to move."

No acknowledgment of him, then. That's how she wanted to play it.

Fine, but he wasn't going down without a fight. "Glad to have you," he said to Tessa. To Meg, he said, "Thought you were still retired."

Meg's gaze flicked to him, away. "I am."

Tessa and Spence exchanged a glance.

Mini Van Damme punched the air in front of him. "Pay up, mister."

Declan did.

After the boy scampered off, Tessa drew out a folded map. She pressed it out on top of one of the enormous pipes, the noise louder here from the moving water inside. Steam hovered down the way, rising from grates in the floor.

"These tunnels run close to the old embassy." She pointed. "We'll follow this one there. "Another tap. "A second will lead us away from the old place and into the new, where I built in a back door."

"Surveillance?" Spence asked.

"Of course," she told them. "Here and here, but we can handle it."

Spence dug in his backpack, bringing out a series of electronics. Each of them received an earbud with a mic and cameras the size of a button to attach to their clothing. Meg waved his offering off. "I've got mine already."

Spence got in her face, studying her eyes. "You got a pair of Eagle Eyes, didn't you? Where's my pair?"

"There was only one in my kit," she told him.

"Show me all entrances and exits," Declan ordered Tessa.

She did, and he committed them to memory, using her map to create his own virtual version. His memory had always been one of his skills.

The last embassy he'd been in was similar in some ways, but each had its own distinct floor plan. "Let's go over tactical requirements for the various scenarios: best case, worse case, holy shit case."

"I'm going in alone," Meg said.

Declan scoffed. "The hell you are."

She pointed to the map and drew an X with her finger. "Spence and Tessa will stay outside the building here to monitor the riot and feed me intel. We need to get Tessa a rifle with a scope so she can be our eyes in the sky while Spence tracks me inside via his phone. You station yourself here." Another X. "If I need help, I'll message you."

Fat chance. He stuck an earbud in and secured the camera on his coat lapel. "We're a goddamn team, Meg. If Flynn wanted you to do this alone, he wouldn't have sent for me and Spence. Grab your gear." He started walking, his insides boiling. Of course, she would try to cut him out of this mission.

She could blame him all she wanted for the past, but he was still a swan and her second in command. "Let's get this over with."

FIVE

If only the Eagle Eye contacts had a "looks could kill" setting. Shoot laser beams. At the very least, freeze assholes who refused to follow orders.

The gadgets of comic books.

She glared at Dec's back as he marched away, shadows swallowing him up. He was a shadow. A goddamn spook in the most literal way.

This was why she'd wanted to get in and out before he and Spence had arrived, but she and Tessa had gotten waylaid by Bruce Lee—the man who ran the underground tunnels like his own personal sovereign state. Nobody went anywhere down here without him knowing about it.

Plus, Tessa had gotten pissy and forced Meg to message Dec with their location. Meg needed Tessa and her blueprints, and letting her down wasn't an option. She had to play nice with Dec.

She'd bought Bruce's silence, along with the aid of

one of his runners, thanks to Tessa's emergency fund. The woman carried an assortment of currency, jewels, and the latest in spyware sewn into her designer outfit, hidden in her thick hair, and strapped to various parts of her body.

The latest iPhone and a ruby ring that had to have cost upwards of three grand had swayed the infamous Lee to offer a deal: his tunnels were available for their use *this once.* If they needed the cover of them again, it would cost double.

Copy that and then some. If all went as planned, this was the one and only time she'd ever be here.

Since her plan had already headed south, thanks to the bear of a brute stalking off without her, odds were slim anything from this point on would go smoothly.

The awkward weight of Tessa and Spence's stares made her skin itch. At least they understood and accepted the chain of command.

Yelling at Dec, who was the best thing she'd seen since everything went to hell, was pointless. He hadn't ended up on Black Swan for nothing. She'd insisted he be one of them. Flynn, for once, had agreed with her choice.

Flynn always used terms like 'dedicated,' 'quick on his feet,' and 'loyal' to describe Dec. In Meg's book, he was all those and more—uncompromising, defiant, and rebellious, bordering on mutinous.

He was also the most rock-steady partner she'd ever had. He never wavered from his values and beliefs. *Predictable,* she told herself, *but maybe that's a good thing.*

Know your enemy was the first thing Flynn had taught her.

Know your friends was the second.

She wasn't sure which category to put Declan Reid in.

Cussing him out might have made her feel better, but she didn't waste time and energy on lost causes anymore. The bubbling brew of shit between them was a pressure cooker bound to explode. Soon, too. She'd take whatever he threw at her once they had the intel and found Tommy, provided he admitted to his own collusion in what had gone down that day with Hagar.

Sucking in her irritation, both at his defiance and the fact he looked so damn good, she met Tessa and Spence's eyes, then jutted her chin at the map. "You heard him."

Marching after her second, she left them scrambling to gather the equipment. They didn't have much, didn't need much, which was typical for their missions. The less stuff, the better. They had to move like cats in the night. Predatory cats. Unseen and unheard.

She jogged to catch Dec before the others could. "You can be an asshole to me all you want once we're done." Seething internally, she still managed to keep her outward expression neutral and unfazed. Her gaze pinned the beam spotlighting their way as they walked side by side. "But right now, I give the orders, and you follow them. Clear?"

His response was barely more than a grunt. "Don't be stupid, Meg. You aren't going in alone. You need me to watch your six."

"Your alpha caveman may believe so, but I'm perfectly capable of taking care of my back, front, and all other sides of me. If things go wrong, I'll call you in, but until you get word from me, you stand down. I don't need to worry about you or them"—she cocked her head to the others, now a yard behind—"getting hurt."

"Flynn told me after the funeral that you'd always bust my balls, but I thought you'd rise above it. Especially in a situation like this. Put the mission above personal feelings for me."

Who was busting whose balls? They swung left, heading in the direction of the former embassy. A turn-of-the-century mansion had been converted into offices and dignitary quarters. The Architect, in her brilliance, had used a long-ago forgotten underground passage, much like the sewers, to connect it to the modern structure now being invaded. That was Meg's way in.

And out.

She hoped. "Insubordination won't be tolerated."

He snorted, his long stride making it difficult for her to keep up. "Fuck that. This team has already lost one member. We're not losing you, too."

Her fingers went to the pendant at her collarbone. The one item she had that had been Jessica's. Grateful that Flynn couldn't see or hear them at the moment because they were underground, she still felt his judgment, as well as Jessie's. Jessie had been a team player and too damn willing to die for her country—one of the reasons the CIA had tried to ensure she didn't. Flynn had counted on Meg to keep her from sacrificing herself.

Meg had failed.

The tunnels were full of sounds that added to its haunting atmosphere. She wasn't concerned with any of those or the ghost stories rampant in Romania about vampires lurking in the shadows. Jessica's spirit, however, seemed to breathe down her neck. "That's not only simplistic reasoning, it's illogical. This situation and the previous one have nothing in common."

One of the reasons Meg was good at her job was because she never assumed any fact was true. While it seemed contrary to logic, throughout history, people had assumed that a belief was fact and fact was reality. Facts were rarely what they appeared to be.

A mission that depended on something that hadn't been verified with her own eyes left a lot of ways things could turn into a goatfuck. The tunnel to the previous embassy could have collapsed. The way in might be impossible to breach, even though it now sat empty. The underground entrance at the new building would definitely be locked and secured. Luckily, Tessa knew the security code—unless it had been changed in the past few months.

A dozen other variables could also cause problems.

Having Dec as her second had always made sense. He was the Holmes to her Watson—cunning, although impulsive, and he had the ability to outsmart everyone, with the exception of her. While she was OCD with details, he was quick on his feet and went with whatever presented itself. He saw the big picture; she broke everything into smaller parts.

She planned for every contingency; he didn't feel the need, constantly adapting in the moment. He provided the team with any and all scenarios because she needed it, not because he did.

It drove her insane.

He drove her insane.

He pulled up short and faced her. "We're the common denominator, Meg. The Black Swans." He lowered his voice. "You and me."

If not for the shadows, she would have sworn his eyes softened when he said it.

Her pulse quickened. Her heart squeezed.

You and me.

How many times had he said that to her during a mission? How many times had she silently repeated it back to him?

"We're part of a team," she corrected. "You need to remember that."

"The way you're acting right now suggests differently. It's okay to rely on others, Meg."

She sucked in a breath. Pinched the pendant between her finger and thumb hard enough to make it hurt. Relying on others meant giving up control. When had that ever worked for her?

The only person she could count on was herself.

But he was right there, alive and breathing, and she'd been so lonely...

So filled with grief.

Self-righteous anger.

"It wasn't your fault," he said, as if reading her mind.

She shoved at the grief and pain, a habit now. They reared their heads every day, and sometimes, it was an exercise in futility to stomp them back into that deep hole she'd dug for them.

But she'd had a lot of practice. "She counted on me. There's no one else to blame."

His expression tightened at that. "We both know you blame me for choosing you over her. Just admit it."

Is that what he thought? In the beginning, yes, she railed at him, the horror of it too much for her to handle. She'd blamed everybody else, even though the therapist reminded her that the person who did the deed was Hagar. He was the killer, not her. Not Dec.

Not Flynn or the CIA.

Not anyone but the terrorist.

It had been meant as a lifeline that the doctor had thrown her, but no matter how she tried to grab hold of it, it slipped through her fingers. The voice in her head said differently, and taunted her every minute of every day. *My fault. My fault. My fault.*

"I should've figured out a way to get you both out," he said.

For a heartbeat, the grief eased. A sensation she'd forgotten flooded through her.

She *wasn't* alone.

He was here, and he understood.

Yes. He, out of all of them, understood. She and Dec had been there, had witnessed what had happened up close and personal. Had shared in the responsibility.

In the aftermath, he'd stormed in. Rescued her as Hagar's death squad helped him escape.

Dec had covered Jessie's body.

In the following weeks, Meg and Dec had tackled the debriefings together. He'd shown up each day for her PT. Had made sure she had groceries in her fridge when she finally went home.

Life. He'd breathed life into her again.

But the oily stickiness of grief would not leave her be. She couldn't handle it. Guilt ate her up. She'd pushed him away. Channeled all of it into hate.

Hate for herself.

Hate for him saving her instead of Jessie.

As he moved closer, helplessness clawed at her throat and burned in her mouth. All the things she'd never said. Those emotions she had kept smothered down in that hole threatening to erupt. A sound came out of her mouth before she could clamp her teeth together.

He grabbed her arm and tugged her to him in an embrace. She froze. Through his jacket, she heard his heartbeat. Strong. Solid. His arms held her up, not allowing her weak legs to crumple.

Muscle memory kicked in, her mind flashing back to all the times she'd allowed him to embrace her. Had welcomed it. Her muscles relaxed, and her mind let go of the need to control.

Life—*living*—flooded her system.

She gasped in a deep breath.

"I've got you," he whispered into her hair. "Like it or not."

Tears burned in her eyes. *Damn it.*

He'd done it to her again. Reduced her carefully constructed barrier to rubble.

The sound of footsteps saved her. She blinked, pushed against his chest to put distance between them. "Yes, well." She dashed at the tear that seeped from the corner of an eye. "Like it or not, I'm still lead on this. One person—me—in and out before anyone realizes it."

Spence and Tessa caught up. "Like Sarajevo," Spence said.

Meg nodded. A clean mission. One of the early ones and the best for BSD. They'd worked together seamlessly because everyone knew their role and stuck to it. "Exactly like that."

"But I know the place like the back of my hand," Tessa argued. "You need me to be your GPS."

She wasn't wrong, but there was no way Meg could risk it. Flynn hadn't okayed her being part of this op and would kick Meg's ass when she returned for involving her. Maybe that was precisely why she *should* take Tessa in with her.

Tessa pointed a finger at Meg's face. "I see that light in your eyes, girl. You know I'm right."

"Let me think on it." They had nearly five kilometers to cover yet. "We need to keep moving."

Two motorbikes waited at the spot Lee had agreed to. Meg hid her surprise that he'd come through but doubted either would start when she looked them over. Pure crap on two wheels. She tried the starter on one. It grunted, turned over, died.

Dec ran his hands over the engine, tracing lines to the brakes, gas tank, headlight. Those hands...she couldn't tear her eyes from them, the way they caressed the bike like a lover.

Dropping to the ground, he fiddled with something under the engine she couldn't see. "Give me some light."

Spence bent and did so. Declan's face was a mix of harsh illumination and thick shadows as he tinkered with something. He slid out and brushed his hands on his jeans. "Try it now."

The tiny beast roared to life.

Still unsettled from his embrace and those words, Meg tried to block them out as he climbed on behind her.

She protested. "You and Spence take the second bike. Tessa rides with me."

"Spence and I together on either of these might be too much," he said over the engine noise.

"Yeah," Spence agreed, helping Tessa on behind him. "But he's at fighting weight, just so you know."

He winked; Declan flipped him the bird.

Whatever that was about.

Throat tight, she ignored her pounding pulse as Dec's muscled thighs framed hers. The tight fit forced him right up against her back. "You sure you don't want me to drive?" he asked in her ear.

Unable to form a snappy comeback, she jetted off down the tunnel as her reply.

Away they went, headlights only creating enough brightness for them to see a few yards at a time. With one arm around her waist, Dec used his flashlight to pick up more. Concentrating was nearly fruitless. His lips next to her ear raised goose flesh on her skin as he issued directions. Her ass sat cradled between his legs. Her pulse raced as fast as the bike at the feel of him snugged up against nearly every part of her.

It's only the mission.

Her adrenaline and pounding pulse could be explained.

She hadn't been undercover in a year.

The last mission had gone to hell.

It was expected that she might be excited.

Yeah, right.

Blowing out a controlled breath, she forced herself to focus.

The five-plus kilometers to the embassy's underground entrance was an obstacle course of people, trash, and junk. They stopped a hundred yards from the connection of the public tunnel to a smaller secondary passage, and left the bikes to hike the rest of the way on foot.

A large slab of metal was hidden behind a deserted pump station. The smell alone was enough to make her gag and hold her breath. No outside force could breach what appeared to be a wall from this side, but on the other side was a security-coded lock.

Tessa cracked her knuckles like a thief about to break into a safe. She trailed a hand along the left side of the metal jamb, eyes closed and lips moving in a silent conversation. Her fingers stopped. She tapped a section of stone. "Here."

Spence yanked out a handheld device. "Give me a minute to access the system and—"

Meg stayed his hand. Tessa drew them back, nodding at Dec. A good thief—a good spy—would take a careful approach, knowing if they damaged the security system, it would trigger alarms. Since this embassy was abandoned, there was no need for finesse. "Shoot it."

He frowned. "The rock here has to be three feet thick, maybe more."

"Nah," Tessa said. "They drilled a hollow trench around the sides and top to run wires for the keypad and cameras. If you hit this spot,"—she pointed where her hand had just been—"the rock will shatter. It's as thin as your phone."

They covered their ears as he pointed his Glock at the spot. It took two bullets, but it did indeed shatter. The second one also blew a hole in the embedded square containing the locking system on the inside. He used a hand to knock bits of stone away, grabbed the box, and yanked it through to their side.

Spence pocketed his device and rubbed his hands together. "Come to Daddy." He jerked wires from their connections and tapped their ends together as if hot-wiring a car. There was a spark, and the door slid open. His smile was triumphant. "Voila."

Once they were all inside, he closed it up again and pulled the box through.

"Disable it," Meg instructed.

He jutted his chin forward in that way of his, telling

her he didn't follow her logic. "What if we have to use this passage as an exit?"

"Our exit strategy is above ground." She scanned the dark hallway. Nothing flashy, but at least it didn't stink. LED lights were spaced at equal intervals. Cameras, too. Flynn and Del were undoubtedly tapped into the embassy's video feed, so she waved. She hit her comm but only heard static. At least Flynn couldn't yell at her.

Yet.

Spence's chin stayed cocked, his brain ready to argue. Declan grabbed the box and jerked the wires out, severing their connection. "I'll take the lead until we reach the entrance."

He took off at a fast clip before she could pull a Spence and argue. She motioned for the others to follow him, suppressing an eye roll while she brought up the rear.

"The new embassy doesn't have a weapons room," Tessa told them. "My best option is to relieve one of the police officers of a rifle."

"You find what you need and get to the building across the street," Meg ordered.

"Roger, that," she said as if she were about to go on a carnival ride. She may have left the Agency for quieter pastures, but the spy she'd been was still inside, hopping with excitement like a junkie who'd fallen off the wagon, anticipating their next fix.

Meg wished she felt that way. For her, all that buzzed in her veins was dread.

SIX

He shouldn't have touched her. She was like a skittish colt, and he'd pushed her too far too fast.

But damn, he hadn't been able to help himself. On the bike, feeling her tucked against him, his arm around her waist, he'd nearly lost control. She smelled of vanilla and cinnamon, with just a hint of some flower he couldn't name. The end of her ponytail had kept brushing across his face, and he'd wanted to bury his nose against her neck, the soft skin there vulnerable and on display to him.

After months of being cut off from her, it had overwhelmed his senses. With only a few layers of material between his dick and her ass, it had been all he could do to keep his phone straight enough for the flashlight to help guide them.

If she'd felt his hardness, she hadn't let on. She hadn't acted affected at all, in fact. She'd remained tense and on alert—as she should have given the circumstances.

But that's exactly what had tipped him off—she was

too tense, too rigid. She wasn't about to admit that she felt anything for him other than loathing.

Maybe he was a fool to believe otherwise.

As they entered the former embassy, nothing but the shell of what it had once been, he forced himself to refocus his thoughts on the task at hand. He couldn't allow the past to matter right now. If they were to succeed, all of them had to be hyperaware.

The empty building was more like a three-story home, and the ghosts of its former employees seemed to hover in the corners. The storms sweeping through the city had lightened only slightly, rivulets of water tracking down the windows.

As they slipped from room to room, dust motes danced in the beams of their phone lights. Whatever security system had been in place was no longer active, but Del and Flynn were once more able to speak to them through their comms.

"Loch Ness, this is Swan One," Meg said, hailing their boss. "We are on approach to the target. Over."

"Swan One, this is Loch Ness," Del responded. "We read you loud and clear and have you in our sites. Over."

"Swan Two, what is your entry plan?" Flynn asked. He wasn't much for radio etiquette.

Tessa responded before Declan could answer. "Through the tunnel between the former embassy and the new one." When the three of them looked at her, she cringed. "Sorry, this is Black Swan...um, Four, I guess? Hey, commander."

Meg looked away. Black Swan Four had been Jessie's designation.

Flynn growled. "Architect, you are to stand down."

Tessa straightened. "You're kidding, right? I'm your ace in the hole."

"You no longer work for me. You cannot be part of this mission, as Swan One knows full well."

There was a message there. Maybe even a threat. Meg didn't seem to care.

Arguing was wasting time. Declan tapped his mike. "This is Swan Two. Entry will be through the tunnel connecting both embassies. Swan One and I will use it to access the target and locate the red bag. Three and The Architect will remain in positions outside. Over."

"Exit plan?" Flynn asked, ignoring his mention of Tessa being involved.

He didn't have one. He had several. Always did. Which their boss knew. He was simply checking off the boxes on his mission list. "Exit plan one, retrace our steps. Exit plan two, use an available ground floor escape route. Exit plan three, rooftop evac."

"That would require a helicopter, or have you developed wings and can fly?"

"Pegasus has been activated, has it not? Over."

Meg narrowed her eyes. She'd believed they'd be on their own once they'd secured the USB.

Flynn chuckled. "On the off chance you do not need a daring rooftop rescue, they'll be stationed three clicks south. Loch Ness will provide the coordinates. You have until sixteen hundred hours to meet up with them. If you blow that window, you'll have to find your own ride home."

He set the timer on his watch. "Roger that."

"Do we still have eyes inside the embassy?" Spence asked.

Del responded. "Hit and miss. Cables have been damaged. At least one server has been destroyed, possibly on purpose by the staff to avoid intel falling into enemy hands. Most sections of the compound have no active security cameras as this point, but we have satellite imagery. The Chief of Mission left yesterday, but there are employees stranded inside."

Could be better, could be worse.

"Loch Ness, we'll keep airwaves open as much as we can," Meg told them, "but may end up going dark if necessary."

"Roger that," Del said.

"Godspeed," Flynn said. "I look forward to buying some of you a drink upon your return."

And kicking the rest of you in the ass, it went without saying.

With that, the comms went silent.

"There was a small armory here in the west wing," Tessa told them. "Should we check it in case anything was left behind?"

"Yeah, let's," Spence said, motioning her to accompany him.

When they'd disappeared, Meg chewed the inside of her cheek, staring into the basement where the next underground trip awaited. "What do you say we call a truce? Just for this mission."

He'd rather have forgiveness, but maybe this was the first step toward that. "The mission comes first."

She gave him a measured glance. "I want your word that if things go belly up like they did previously with Hagar, you will not put me ahead of the others."

So that's what she meant by a truce.

He couldn't do that. "I thought you were the leader."

"I am, and that's my order."

Arguing with her was stupid, but he couldn't help himself. "A team without its leader is not a team. The success of the mission depends on you. Every one of us knows that and accepts it. Jessie did, too. "

She raised a hand as if to shield herself from his words. "From here on out, we do not speak of her. Not until this is over and everyone is safe back at Langley. The stakes are too high."

She was right. Their total attention had to be on the present, not the past. He gave a resentful nod. "A truce until we're all back on US soil. Then, you and I are going to have it out. Once and for all."

He dug a flat, black carrier from his jacket pocket and laid it on one of the dusty desks. As he unzipped it and brought out the contents, he felt her slip up behind him.

"What is all that?" she asked.

"Spence isn't the only kid with a bag of magic tools." He picked up a sleek, silver device, slightly bigger than a lipstick tube. "Meet Vishie IV, the latest development in mini-lasers, courtesy of Del and R&D."

"Looks like a kitchen torch. Does it melt things?"

She'd probably enjoy that. She always had a thing for fire. "It's a non-lethal laser designed to temporarily blind targets. Aim, fire, and they're blinded long enough for you to make a move. Won't cause permanent damage, just enough to impair their vision up to five minutes."

She twisted the tube, inspecting it. Then held it up and fired the laser using the button on the side of the wall. The beam flashed a strobe of colors on the dingy paint. "And the range?"

"Effective up to twenty feet," he told her. "Less than three, and you'll risk burning your target's retina."

She nodded, twisting it closed and slipping it into the pocket of her army green jacket. That damn thing.

He couldn't believe she still wore it but understood the significance. It had belonged to her dad, a former Delta force member. He'd died before he got to see his only daughter graduate from The Farm and become one of the CIA's most trusted and valuable weapons.

Meg was always collecting souvenirs of those she'd loved and lost.

"What else?" she asked, fingering what looked like a compact handgun with an unusual muzzle.

He handed it to her. "Ultrasonic weapon. It will admit a targeted, high-frequency soundwave that disrupts the inner ear. The target will feel nauseous and disoriented and may even end up incapacitated. Perfect for crowd control and close quarters, and while the effect is nearly instantaneous, it's short-lived, so timing is everything."

She gave him a look that suggested she wanted to use

it on him. He grinned, letting her know he could read her mind and knew she never would do it. He placed a set of earplugs to protect herself from the weapon.

She found a place for those and the weapon. "Where are your toys?"

He tucked the bag away and patted his own pockets. "We get in, grab the USB, and get out."

"Ghosts," she agreed. "Although, for the record? You should let me do this."

Spence and Tessa returned, disappointment written on their faces. "Not even a swizzle stick left," Spence said. "Bloody wankers could've left us something."

Tessa scanned the grouping of desks. "Check under every drawer and behind every file cabinet. There's got to be some forgotten, hidden gun here somewhere. This place wasn't simply phased out. It was shut down in a twenty-four-hour period. Everyone moved to the new embassy in a rush."

"Why?" Spence asked.

"A group of unhappy nationalists decided to stage a protest and let us know," Meg told him.

Tessa nodded. "It was in our best interests to make the move quickly and efficiently." She began checking under the nearest desk. "Which is why I'm guessing a few things might have been forgotten."

"We don't have time for a thorough search," Declan said. "We move now and use what we've got."

Tessa and Spence looked at Meg.

He held his breath, waiting for her to override the order. He could see it in her eyes—the desire to do it, even though it was exactly what she wanted the others to do.

He quirked a brow. *Truce, remember?*

Her gaze darted away, and well, would you look at that—she gave a nod of confirmation.

Spence headed for the basement, his boots pounding down the stairs. "Comms might be spotty. We'll do our best to cover you."

The basement floor was stone and smelled of mildew and rot. A rodent had died in the corner, its bones stark against the damp foundation.

A rusted metal door was somewhat camouflaged behind a shelf on wheels, containing a few random office supplies left behind. "That's it," Tessa said. "That's the egress to the passageway."

It was locked and covered with cobwebs. Declan knocked them away and contemplated the electronic keypad. Could he shoot this one, too, to gain access, or would destroying it also destroy their chances of entry?

"I've got it," Spence said, digging out his phone. He tapped at the screen, bringing it close to the keypad.

"The batteries might be dead," Meg said.

"These are muli-use." Spence waved his phone around the top and bottom. "They can use electricity but also have an internal battery in case of a power outage."

"I didn't design this entry, but smart locks have been around for a while." Tessa grinned as they heard the thunk of a deadbolt slamming back. "And they have a manual override."

Dec motioned Spence back and listened. No sound

came from the other side. The hinges groaned when he pulled the metal open, keeping his frame a shield just in case. He didn't expect a surprise, but best to anticipate one anyway.

Only darkness met his eyes. Total nothingness, as if he were blind.

The odors of mildew and dead things stuffed their way up his nose. Far off in the distance, he picked up faint sounds. The rioting? This passage was acting like a funnel for the noise.

Meg squeezed in beside him. "We need night vision."

He fished out his phone and thumbed on the flashlight. "We'll make do."

A much smaller tunnel came into view—almost too small. He wouldn't be able to walk standing up.

Tessa made a face as the wave of rot and mold hit her. "Gross."

"Be ready for anything," Meg said, stepping across the threshold. "Without security cameras and no way of knowing who or what might have been exploring this place regardless of that lock, we might run into a surprise or two."

Declan followed, ducking his head. "Surprises are what we do best."

The absolute darkness felt like a suffocating blanket, the air so stagnant it made breathing difficult. The passage was pure stone, carved out centuries ago. It grew narrower, forcing him to turn sideways at various points to get his shoulders through. Spence had to do the same.

Meg took his phone and forced them to slow as she

peeked around a bend. A rat scurried by, disturbed by the light, and she jumped.

"God, I hate rats," Spence said.

Tessa watched the thing disappear into the gloom. "Pocket dogs are highly intelligent and capable of forming emotional bonds with their owners. They have excellent memories, can handle complex tasks, and show empathy toward other animals."

An odd silence fell as they all stared at her.

She shrugged. "What?"

"Pocket dogs?" Spence echoed.

"Out of all of that, that's what you got?" She rolled her eyes.

Declan grabbed the phone. Meg held on. "Let me scout ahead," he said to her.

"No." She wouldn't let go. "We stay together, no matter what, until we get to the embassy."

Damn bullheaded woman.

Water dripped from a crack in the bend as she continued on, turning her back on him. A portion of the wall had crumbled, filling their path with mud and stones.

"Surprise number one," Spence muttered.

"Don't suppose you have a shovel in your bag of magic tricks," Meg muttered to Declan.

"We'll have to go back," he said. "We'll look for a tool to dig our way through."

She climbed the hill of mud, shining the light through a tiny opening at the top of the debris. "I can squeeze through." Turning, she flipped him the phone and pulled out hers, flicking on its light. "This is where we part ways."

"The hell we do," he said.

Spence reached for her. "Meg, don't you dare!"

Tessa shimmied out of her bulky jacket, pushing it through behind Meg, flashing both men a grin over her shoulder, and flopping onto all fours to follow.

Declan growled loud enough to startle another rat, gripping Tessa by the ankles and hauling her back. "Fuck that. Meg!" he yelled through the opening, spotting her in the light bouncing off the walls beyond the mudslide. "Get your ass back here."

"When I have the USB," she told him. "Ghosts, remember? In and out. Be ready to join me at the evac site."

He stretched an arm toward her, his head clipping one of the overhead rocks. "We're a team, goddammit. We do this together."

The light faded to nothing as she gave him one last glance and took off running.

SEVEN

Leaving her team behind was best for all of them. That's what she told herself as Dec's yells faded away.

She raced along the ever-shrinking passageway, assuring herself that she could move more quickly and efficiently without them. Keeping them safe was her highest priority, even above getting the red bag.

Protecting them had always been a high priority, but she hadn't realized until they were closing in on the embassy that it had become her number one goal.

This tunnel had to be centuries old, and she wondered what it had initially connected to and who had used it all those years ago. Her heart felt as stuck in a time warp as it was, slowly disintegrating under the weight of the present.

She didn't suffer from allergies, but the heavy rot was causing her eyes to water and her nose to run. Following the winding path, she came upon another partial landslide of stones that forced her to crawl on hands and knees to squeeze past it.

She clawed at the ground with her free hand, the memory of Declan's embrace flashing through her mind. To be held again felt foreign, and yet her body ached for another chance to sink into his solidness.

He'd forced her carefully constructed walls to crumble, and she hadn't been able to repair them fast enough. Offering the truce had been a Hail Mary—her only way to shield herself against the flood of emotions seeing him and hearing him insist he still didn't regret saving her over Jessie had caused.

The damp earth clung to her clothes, and she cleared the rockslide, the air so thick her lungs struggled to suck in enough oxygen. The sounds of the rioting were still muffled but growing louder.

The tunnel forked, and she stopped, pointing her light in each direction and recalling Tessa's paper map. There hadn't been any alternate branches, she was sure of it. *Which way?*

All these damn choices with no sure outcomes. She was sick of them. Why couldn't anything be clear-cut? Why couldn't she find clarity?

A boom exploded off in the distance, causing her to throw up her arms as dirt and debris rained down on her. Dust filled the air, and she heard the screech of rats as they jetted by her feet. She waved away the clogged air, looking to her right. That's where it had originated.

What the hell were they doing up there, blowing up the embassy?

Covering her mouth with the crook of her elbow, she started running again. She kept her pace steady, fearing the explosion might have caused her access point to be cut off. The moderate glow of the flashlight showed a few minor rock slides here and there as she navigated along, but nothing substantial enough to stop her.

The ground began to rise, and the tunnel widened again. Lowering her arm, she checked the air and found it more breathable.

Up ahead, she saw the end of the line, a rusted metal ladder embedded in the wall, leading up to a manhole.

That hadn't been on Tessa's map, either. Meg pocketed her phone and began climbing.

She stopped on each rung, testing her weight on the ladder, knowing it could pop free from the stone in a heartbeat. The last thing she needed was to end up on her ass with the heavy ladder on top of her, injured and alone.

Dec's voice played loud in her head. *This is why you always have a partner. We are a team.*

The principal was one she had pounded into all of their heads on every mission. But Jessie had been her partner on the last one, and look what it had gotten her.

She took another step up, the metal groaning. Pausing, she gave the ladder a tiny jiggle. She was still close enough to the ground that if she fell, it wouldn't be bad.

The thing held, and she went up another rung. By the time she got to the middle, she could hear pieces of the rock wall falling to the ground. She hoped she wasn't about to join them.

Even when she neared the top, she didn't breathe a sigh of relief. Slowly and carefully, she removed her phone and shone the light on the covering over her head. More rusty metal with a handle. She was unsure if it was a true manhole that led to a street or if this was the access point to the new embassy. It was heavy, and she doubted it had been opened in the last decade, if not a century.

She tested the handle and shoved, bracing her legs on the ladder and praying it held.

The metal under her groaned; the metal above her refused to move.

Sweat trickled down her neck and under her collar. Another reason she could have used Dec's brute strength. His weight might've been too much for the ladder, though.

...fighting weight...

Hmm. Was he still taking out his stress in the ring?

Putting the phone away, she took a couple of deep breaths and tightened all her muscles. Giving a grunt, she thrust all her weight at the metal cover again.

A screech, a shift.

Too bad it wasn't enough.

Again, she hit it with all her might.

It moved two inches this time.

But the ladder shuddered under the pressure.

Panting, she wiped sweat from her brow and shook out her hands.

Dec and the others were probably digging through that first mudslide. Another few minutes and they would catch up with her. She'd never hear the end of it.

This was all Hagar's fault. The goddamn bastard.

Focusing on the rage she carried for him, she felt a shot of adrenaline flood her system. She would not let him defeat her. Would not let him put her team in danger again.

Gathering all her strength and balance, she propelled her hands into the rusty metal, lunging at it as hard as she could.

Dim light seeped around the edges as she managed to lift the disk. The sounds of rioting hit her, along with yelling and glass breaking. The pungent odor of burning wood and melting plastic assaulted her nose.

So did the stringent scent of cleaning products.

Her legs trembled at the strain, her biceps screaming. It was now or never. She gathered herself one more time and *shoved*.

The metal slid across the floor.

Relieved, she sagged, but only for a few seconds.

No one peered down at her. No shouts rang out, alerting others. All she saw as she stared up was rows of cleaning products on wire shelves and a light fixture overhead.

Hauling herself up through the hole, she ran into several mop buckets. Edging them out of the way, she swung her legs around, nailing a cart filled with cleaning supplies and rubber gloves. It had wheels and rolled into a pair of overalls on a hook. Boxes of napkins, paper towels, and toilet paper were on another shelf opposite her.

The janitor's closet.

Beyond the door, she heard a scream. Rushing footsteps.

That scream...

At her core, she wanted to help people. It was who she was. She didn't get off on power or accomplishments. She'd joined the CIA to fight against injustice and inequality.

She saved people, not killed them.

Deep down, she wanted to help each and every one of those still stuck inside the embassy. She'd known coming in that the riot was bad, but she hadn't considered just how bad. The explosion earlier might have allowed Hagar to breach the double layer of gates. If he and his death squad were here...

All those trapped inside would be dead soon.

Her gut cramped.

Move. She crept across the floor, inventorying the chemicals lining the shelves. One never knew when they might need to create their own bomb.

Pressing her ear against the door, she listened to the chaos on the other side. If Hagar and his men, or any of the citizens they had recruited to riot, were inside the embassy, it would make everything harder.

Be a ghost. That's what she was good at, and that's why she was here.

It was one thing to avoid the rioters; another to avoid the embassy's security detail. They would already be running on pure adrenaline and would shoot first and ask questions later.

This was one of the reasons Dec had outfitted her

with the laser and ultrasonic weapon—she needed to be able to disable them without causing any permanent damage.

Muffled voices came from the other side, with urgent conversations and more running footsteps. Her comm gave a burst of static, making her jump, and Del's voice came through. "Black Swan One, this is Loch Ness. Do you read? Over."

She had to assume that the tech guru was also picking up what Eagle Eyes showed him. Flynn would know shortly that she had ditched the rest of her team.

Didn't matter. She was already on his shit list.

And his was his own damn fault for reactivating her.

Before she slipped out into the hallway, she stole the badge hanging on the uniform. She probably wouldn't need it, but better safe than sorry. "Loch Ness, this is Swan One. You're coming through loud and clear. I am inside the embassy. Over."

In the corridor, the air was thick with the stench of sweat and fear, and mingled with the acrid bite of smoke. Flickering emergency lights cast shadows along the carpeted floors and walls decorated modestly with landscape paintings that now hung askew or had crashed to the floor. It gave the whole place an eerie, post-apocalyptic feel.

"Roger that," Del said. "Eagle Eyes not receiving, but picking you up on security cameras above you."

Moving quickly and quietly, she checked one of the posted maps at the end of the hall, where it split left and right. An occasional crash punctuated the distant hum of panicked voices as desperate employees tried to barricade themselves against the unfolding chaos.

It was Flynn's voice she heard next. "Where the hell is your team, Swan one?"

She didn't lie. "There was a cave-in. I was the only one who got through the tunnels."

A heavy pause came back to her.

The voices of two men sounded behind her, and she ducked into the analyst department. The large, central room was a maze of overturned furniture and scattered papers.

Controlling her breathing as she heard them turn down in the opposite direction, she froze when a security guard's radio squawked. A woman shouted in the distance for help, and he took off running.

Again, Meg felt the itch to help, but she knew she couldn't. The mission had to come first. Once she had the USB in her greedy little hands, though, she would do what she could.

"The safe is on the second floor," Del told her, "inside the Chief of Mission's office in the southwest corner."

Giles Marchetti was a Senior Foreign Service Officer at the US Department of State with twenty-some years of experience in diplomacy and national security. He'd been after the Romanian embassy job for ten years and had the language skills, diplomatic experience, and all-around magnetism to land it when it was finally open.

She cracked open the door and let herself out into the hall once more. "Heading that direction now."

Here and there, she had to duck into other offices, a

women's bathroom, and the lunchroom to avoid various staff members. She spotted another guard, this one stumbling around with a bloody sleeve and his gaze darting around wildly. "You there," he yelled at her. "What are you doing? Everyone is supposed to be gathering in the health center."

The embassy had a health center? Was that a sophisticated term for a gym? "On my way," she lied.

Her fingers automatically brushed the grip of the ultrasonic weapon, its presence reassuring and sobering. She didn't want to use it against anyone who might be an ally, but he didn't know she was on his side. He'd probably already encountered intruders, and she was another threat in his eyes.

She flashed him the janitor's badge. "I was trying to help some of the others first. How's your arm?"

There was a cut on his forehead, leaking blood into his left eye. He brushed at it and waved off her question. "I'm fine. Turn around and head to the gym."

Yep, just as she'd thought.

A woman limped around the corner, sobbing and clutching a framed photo to her chest. The guard went to help her, and Meg did the same, getting both of them to the stairwell door.

As it closed, she pivoted and ran toward her intended target, double-checking the directions posted on every corner and following the arrows. Marchetti's office was in sight when she heard a voice shout, "Stop! Stop, or I'll shoot!"

It wasn't a guard, but a man dressed in a suit. His

voice was tight and demanding, his adrenaline surging. He raised a weapon, eyes narrow with suspicion.

She showed him her hands, attempting to appear non-combative. All she needed was to get shot before she even made it to Marchetti's. "I'm here to help."

He hesitated, grip tightening on the stock. "Prove it."

"You don't have time for this," Flynn barked at her. "Del will—"

Static filled her ear, and she tapped the comm.

The man, thinking she was going for a weapon, fired.

As she dove for the floor, bullets rained down...

EIGHT

Declan's heart stopped when he heard the gun go off.

Not just once, but four goddamn times.

He'd been trailing Meg and had come upon the scene just as the suit fired on her.

Debris flew from where the bullets embedded themselves in the wall.

Declan raised his own weapon, bringing the butt down on the back of the man's head.

The suit slumped to the floor, unconscious, and he had to calm the rage he felt so he didn't put a bullet in the man's chest.

It wasn't his fault; it was the Black Swan leader curled into a ball on the floor. Declan rushed to her, scanning for wounds.

Not a drop of blood marred her skin or clothes. Just a healthy amount of dirt and sweat. She shoved his roving hands away as she sat up. "Nice timing."

"He could have killed you. Where are your weapons?"

She brushed at the dusty fragments, adding a layer of grime to her already dirty self. "He was scared but not dangerous, as evidenced by the fact he fired into that wall and not me."

In his ear, Flynn demanded an update. The camera in the upper corner was lights out, so they didn't have eyes on this area.

Meg responded, shooting Declan a glare. "This is Swan One, over. Swan Two has joined me, and we're on our way to the safe." She gestured for him to follow, and he had to stuff down all that rage, making his nerves tingle. This was no time for hurt feelings. "Is Marchetti's office locked?"

Dell came back with an affirmative, but also reassurance. "It's open. Although the Chief of Mission is out of town, someone has entered his office. Could be the DCM."

Marchetti's deputy chief. Whatever he said next was dampened by static.

"You fucking left me," Declan snarled.

Meg muted her comm and signaled him to do the same as she headed for the office. "I made a decision. I could fit through the opening, and you couldn't. Time is slipping away, and I knew you would catch up with me as soon as you could clear the mudslide. It wasn't personal."

Like hell it wasn't. Reinstating his comm, he marched past her, finding the Chief of Mission's corner office and flinging open the door. Seething. He was seething.

This was what she fucking did to him.

A grizzled man, whose white shirt and tie were rumpled and stained with sweat, whirled from a spot behind the desk, papers in hand. The sound of a shredder droned as it ate up documents.

His eyes darted between Meg and Declan, suspicion etched deep in his wrinkled face. "Who the hell are you?"

Meg scanned the room, dismissing him. Her comm was now active, too, but all they were getting was more static. "Where is the safe?"

Declan looked for the man's ID. It was missing. "You the Deputy Chief?"

"I doubt that's any of your business." His nervous gaze took in Declan's size and the weapon on his waistband. "I don't want any trouble."

"What are you doing in here?"

"Cleaning up this goddamn mess."

Del's voice cut through the static. "...Hagar...to breech...front..."

"Finish what you're doing," Megan instructed. "And hurry. Time is running out before the terrorists overrun this place."

"Terrorists?" the man sputtered. "What terrorists?"

"State sent us," Declan told him. "We're here for a USB that's inside the safe. We need access, and we need it now."

The man's attention flickered to a large painted picture at the far end of the room. It looked like he was about to deny knowing anything, but the sound of gunfire erupted outside, echoing like thunder in the room. He ducked behind the desk.

"Got it." Meg marched to the credenza, removed the framed pictures, and surveyed the electronic box behind it. "Loch Ness, are you there? A retina scan and thumbprint are required for the safe."

This time, it was Tessa who came across the comms. "Nothing to worry about. Loch Ness told me your Eagle Eyes are programmed for the retina scan, and Swan Two has a glove with the required thumbprint."

Declan joined Meg, fishing out the glove. "Well, what do you know? All right, eye scan first."

"Tap in this combo of numbers," Tessa said, reeling them off, "Then hold still."

Meg followed her instructions, and they both froze as the scanner did its thing. The light switched to green, and a soft automated female voice said, "Retina scanned confirmed. Hello, Deputy Chief. Please place your thumb on the indicated scanner."

The man popped his head above the desk's hiding place. "I have a bypass key."

"Now you tell us," Declan growled.

He stood, crinkling paper in his fists. "I had to be sure you're who you say you are. You haven't even shown me any ID."

The latex glove felt too tight against Declan's skin, even though it was as thin as his epidermis. He adjusted the fit before placing his digit in the slot. "Go back to your shredding. We've got this."

In unison, he and Meg held their breath until they

heard the voice say, "Thumbprint scan accepted." A click sounded, and Meg grabbed the handle.

A fresh burst of gunfire echoed outside the room. The man dropped the last of his papers and ran.

The safe was as tall as Declan and twice as deep. Too narrow for him to comfortably walk inside, but big enough for Meg.

She ducked into the interior, a motion sensor turning on a single LED light. Shelves lined the walls, filled with boxes and metal cases that appeared meticulously organized.

Empty spots revealed certain items had been removed. By the chief?

Declan knew she was asking herself the same question. "Why didn't he take that?" she asked softly, pointing to a leather pouch on the second shelf marked classified.

Their red bag.

Stripping off the glove, he jammed it into his pocket. He needed more light. His phone once more did the job, and he ran the beam over everything, catching her in it. "Check the contents."

She snatched it up and unzipped it. Her face fell. Opening the pouch wide, she held it up for him to see. His gut sank when he spotlighted the interior.

The *empty* interior.

A string of curses flew from his mouth.

They began to rifle through everything else on the shelves. There were other pouches to unzip and search, boxes of paper files, and a metal box with a flimsy lock that Declan busted using the butt of his gun. It contained stacks of various currencies.

A collection of metal cases for transporting handguns and various tech equipment came next. One of the guns was gone, the outline of it in foam inside the case, suggesting the chief had also taken the silencer it came with. All the equipment was still there—listening devices, two-way radios, military-grade night vision goggles. On the top shelf rested a rifle in its gun case.

But not one goddamn USB.

From the front of the building came an explosion and hysterical screams. Plaster rained down from the ceiling, and pictures fell from the walls, crashing to the floor and adding to the already ravaged office. The rifle fell, hitting Meg in the head and knocking her off balance.

He grabbed her as she stumbled into him. "That came from the main lobby."

She rubbed her head and looked sick. "Hagar has made it past the gates, brick walls, and blown the front entrance."

"We're about to have company. Time for us to bail."

Their eyes met for a brief moment. If he didn't know better, he would have thought there was gratitude in hers. It was probably just the lighting.

Or his desperate imagination.

She drew away. "Someone knew what was on that USB. They took it and that gun with the silencer, but left the rest. Even the cash."

"They were in a panic," he said, considering the motivation behind such a move, "and they needed to move quickly. Couldn't carry too much and felt threatened enough to arm themselves."

"And it was someone who had access to this safe."

"The chief or deputy chief."

Her chin cocked in the direction where the man had exited. "Or that guy, whoever he is." She tried to raise Del. Got nothing but static.

He looked toward the open door, wondering how far the guy had managed to get.

Intel could be used to bribe, coerce, and threaten. To blackmail and to intimidate. "What if our thief took it for another reason?" he asked.

"Like what?" As if reading Declan's mind, Meg sucked in knowing breath. "You think Marchetti is a traitor?"

"Not the chief." Declan motioned for her to follow him. "The man doing the shredding."

Tessa suddenly joined in the conversation. "What the hell is on that USB?" she muttered.

Meg followed him across the room and hit her comm. "Loch Ness, we have a problem."

Flynn's voice cut through the static. "Then solve it."

"I can't."

Declan sent her a look suggesting she remember they were a team.

She corrected herself as she waited for him to scan the hall before they went in pursuit of their target. "*We* can't."

"Why not?" Flynn snapped.

"Because, sir, the bag is here, but the USB isn't."

"Loch Ness, this is Swanny Three," Spence cut in. "We have more problems than that. Are you getting this on your feed?"

"What is it?" Declan demanded, ignoring radio protocol.

"The front entrance is wide open," Spence told them. "The police are nowhere in sight, and Hagar and the death squad are swarming the building."

He knew it took all Meg's willpower to ask the next question. "Orders?"

Nothing but silence followed.

Until...

"Get out," Flynn ordered. "Abort now."

NINE

The mission was a failure.

Blown.

Hagar was inside.

Coming for her.

For them.

Meg reeled in her panicked thoughts. There was no way the terrace could know she was here, that the Black Swans were here. Her team.

Hagar *wasn't* coming for her, he was coming for something else.

But what? The USB?

Looked like he was going to be as disappointed as she was.

She muted her comm and spoke to Dec as they snuck down the hall, heading back the way they had come. "Are we sure Hagar is after the USB? He's a showman, but inciting a riot? He's more likely to bride someone to get that intel, isn't he?"

Dec touched his earbud, muting his comm as well. "You heard our orders. We're leaving."

"We don't have the USB or Tommy." Was Hagar after him? If the terrorist bastard had done his homework, he would know Tommy was gone. "Does Hagar already have him? Does Tommy know what's on the drive?"

"Meg," Declan grumbled, "we're not pursuing it further unless ordered."

They moved swiftly, weaving through the chaotic halls. "We have to find Shredder Man." She pulled up short, knowing what she had to do. "We might be able to save the mission."

He gave a terse huff, stopping as well. Raking a hand over his face, he shook his head and met her eyes for a brief, condemning moment. "Knew you'd say that."

"You need to find the gymnasium. There's a bunch of employees there and they will need help evacuating. Hagar no doubt has the place completely surrounded, so you'll have to take them out through the tunnels."

"And let you have all the fun going after our shredding expert? I don't think so."

Her hands went to her hips. "I thought we understood who was in charge of this mission."

"Hagar loves to be on stage, and we know how he enjoys taking hostages as prisoners, but only if he controls the environment. There are probably fifty, if not more, in this place—too many for him to control or move."

"He might simply shoot them all. We have to evacuate them."

"We can't get fifty people to the tunnel and out of here without making them sitting ducks."

They were all sitting ducks at the moment. "I'll keep Hagar and his men distracted. He's not expecting me to be here, and I'd bet he'll find me equally attractive to whatever he's after."

The way Declan looked at her told her she was a distraction, even for him. It wasn't the same kind, but she saw the heat flare in his eyes at the term.

She hit her comm. "Loch Ness, we're going after the USB. The possible thief is still in the building."

Only static answered. She pointed toward the hall leading to the stairs. "Get those people out. I'll catch up with you when I can."

If I can.

Dec gave her a humorless smile. "When will you learn that you cannot get rid of me? The last time we divided up the team, we lost one of our members. Granted, there are times and certain missions when that makes sense. This isn't one of them." He flicked his wrist over to check his watch. "We need to be at that evac site in two hours. I'm not here to play the hero and save all those people, but for you, I'll do it."

She was confused—was he going to lead the trapped staffers to the tunnel or not? "I don't need a hero. What I need is someone who follows orders."

"Blah blah blah. Heard it before. Do you know why I'm your second?"

"Because of your qualifications."

"Because our boss assigned me the position in order

to keep you from taking extreme risks beyond what's necessary for the parameters of every mission."

It was as if someone had thrown ice water over her head. "What?"

"I've never seen your file, but my orders from the highest levels of Langley have always been to keep you in check. You are one of the most valuable assets they've had in recent years. I am their insurance that you come back after every mission."

Her legs went weak, and she had to put a hand against the wall. "You bastard. Were you ever going to tell me?"

He strutted past her for the stairs that would take him to the main entrance. "Save it. You can kick me off your team later. For now, I'm going after Hagar, and you're going after the USB."

She reached for the stewing anger that had kept her from dissolving into misery for so many months, but it wasn't there. The bleak nothingness devoured her instead. All this time...

She'd thought Dec balanced her out. When Flynn had given her the responsibility for picking her team...

He'd fed Declan Reid to her.

Because he wanted him to be her bodyguard.

A flicker of anger fired up her limbs, and her feet started moving. She jogged to catch up with Dec as he hit the stairwell down. She grabbed him by the back of the jacket, stopping him three steps from the landing, and forced him to face her. "I thought you chose me over her because of our relationship. Why didn't you tell me you were simply following orders?"

He moved up one step, putting himself nose to nose with hers. His lowered voice came out with a cutting edge to it. "I *did* choose you because of our relationship." He came up another step, towering over her and forcing her to step back. "I will *always* choose you, regardless of my orders."

Before she could say a word, he brought his mouth down on hers.

His lips were warm and demanding. Possessive.

She was immune to many things, but Declan's lips were not one of them. Even now, after his confession, those lips could bring her to her knees.

She shoved at his chest, fighting to move away. He allowed it, both of them breathing heavily as their eyes stayed locked on each other's.

He reached out as if he would grasp her arms and drag her back, but then he let them fall to his sides. "I've wanted to do that for a long time."

She wanted to slap his face, yell about how inappropriate his timing was, not to mention the fact that nonconsensual kisses were rude and...

She swallowed hard and licked her lips, watching his eyes track the movement. Screw that. All of it. His touch, his lips—she wanted more. More of his steadiness. More of...him.

I will always choose you...

"I shouldn't be here," she admitted. "My head is... Screwed up."

She thought he might reach for her again, but he didn't. "No more so than the rest of the world. No matter what happens, we are a team. I won't let you go off the deep end, but you have to let me help you."

There was a part of her that wanted to throw her arms around his neck, to throw caution—and her damaged, broken heart—to the wind.

Later.

She hoped there would be time for that later.

Always reading her mind, he held out of hand. "Don't let Hagar see you. I'll distract him." *And end him if given the opportunity.* It was in his eyes, if not said aloud. "You focus on that USB."

She slipped her hand into his. "If we get separated..."

"I'll meet up with you and the others at the evac site."

"Be careful."

Their footsteps were silent as they descended, and once they reached the fire door on the first floor, Dec insisted she stay put while he scouted ahead. It killed her to allow him to take the lead, but he was much better at stealth than she was. She was more likely to double-fist her weapons and start taking out any terrorist she ran into.

Which would only make matters worse, but God, it would feel good to get at least a little revenge on the men who had kidnapped her, tortured her, and did even worse to her friend.

She paced while she waited, the ultrasonic gun in hand in case anyone came through the door that wasn't him. A minute grew into three, then five. She was ready to ignore his orders and go after him when he slipped back into the stairwell, a finger to his lips.

He leaned in and spoke into her ear, his breath warming the shell. "There are at least a dozen, if not more. Right now, they're looting, along with a bunch of the citizens who joined the uprising. Hagar is watching. It's as if he's waiting for something."

"Or someone," she whispered back. "Did you spot Shredder Man?"

"Negative. But Hagar's lieutenant, Sayed Karzai, mentioned *finding the rat*, if my Farsi is still accurate."

He wasn't fluent in it, but better than she was. "Could be our guy."

A shrug. "Or anyone else. We can't search everyone in the place, but maybe Shredder Guy is Marchetti's assistant and took the drive to hide it. We need to find out."

"He may be armed with the missing weapon. We just didn't see them on his person."

He handed her his Sig. "Fully loaded. Don't take chances. If anyone, including that other trigger-happy moron, lifts so much as an eyebrow at you, shoot them."

She pushed it away. "You need that more than I do."

"Meg." He held it out. "Either you take this, or I stick to you like glue."

She worried her bottom lip. "You are always so bullheaded."

He snorted a laugh. "Pot, kettle, on that one, sweetheart."

Accepting the weapon, she checked the safety and flipped it off. "What's your plan to distract Hagar?"

"Thought I'd take out a few of his men to warm up, then confront the SOB to his face."

Her stomach crawled. "Swans do not cause a spectacle."

"You can fire me once we're back on US soil."

She narrowed her eyes. "I might do that anyway."

He flicked the end of her nose. "I welcome the challenge." Opening the door, he gestured for her to follow. "On three."

She held her breath as he counted and then they were racing down a central corridor toward the building's once beautifully appointed entrance and bright foyer.

As they reached a set of double doors behind the main reception area, Dec held up a hand for her to stop. One of the doors stood cracked open as if someone had just run through it.

Meg's heart raced as she peered through the slit, hearing raised voices, the splintering of wood, and the crunching of glass. People milled about, bent on destroying every last plant, picture, table, and chair. Through the melee, she caught sight of the man who terrorized her dreams.

Mosai Hagar stood in the center of the lobby atop a glass and steel coffee table, surveying his handiwork. The front doors were missing, an open maw to the world outside, the protestors rushing in and out.

Three armed men flanked him, all of them keeping their beady gazes on who and what entered the embassy.

As he felt the weight of her gaze, he swiveled, looking directly at her.

Dec jerked her back, but not before she saw Hagar smile.

The walls and ceiling began to close in on her. A weight crushed against her chest. She couldn't breathe.

There was no way he knew it was her. No way he knew she was here or that the sliver of her that he had seen revealed her identity.

And yet, even in that split second, it felt as if he had looked directly into her soul.

The image of Jessie on her knees flashed in front of her. That same look he'd given Meg had been on his face, then—a horrible, pure evil smile as he brought the machete down...

She stumbled as Dec hustled her down the corridor. A lifeline. Her lifeline.

"One foot in front of the other," he murmured as he kept her close, only stopping when they were around the corner. He pressed her against the wall, staring into her eyes. "I won't let anything happen to you. Not this time."

She clung to him and renewed her vow—for Jessie and herself. *I will get revenge on Hagar, one way or another.*

TEN

Declan's ears roared with his pulse, seeing the recognition in Hagar's eyes when he'd spotted Meg through the few inches of open door. How could he have known it was her? He couldn't have seen enough of her face to make her.

And here she was, eyes wide, body trembling, breathing in gulps.

He wanted to punch the wall. Punch Hagar. Instead, he kept a steadying grip on her shoulders. "I'll handle him once we retrieve what we came for. Just breathe, Meg."

She did, keeping her focus on him. In and out, he breathed with her.

Determination hardened her pretty eyes. She still leaned against the wall, trembling, but said, "He's mine."

He knew what she meant, even though he didn't like it. She wasn't a vigilante, and while she had the skills to take out any terrorist or criminal if necessary, this act would be far too personal for her ever to come back from.

She stiffened. "Listen." She pointed back toward the lobby. Hagar's men were shouting for the crowd to disperse. A smattering of gunfire went off, and people started screaming. "What are they doing?"

What, indeed. Why hadn't Hagar sent his goons after Meg?

Going against all his instincts, Declan released her and stole around the corner toward the double doors. They were still open a crack, and he watched the crowd scrambling out the gaping hole in the front. Only Hagar and his men remained.

Except for a familiar face—Shredder Man.

"We've been looking for you, Mr. Anderson," Hagar said, dark, merciless eyes locking on the guy as another of his squad shoved the assistant forward.

Anderson stumbled and fell to his knees before raising his hands in surrender. His slacks and shirt were torn and bloody now. His hair was matted with sweat and dirt. "I told you, I don't know where he is. He's not here. You're wasting your time."

Meg sidled up next to him, and Declan was torn. Should he force her to leave, take the tunnel and escape, or keep listening?

She scrunched her brows as Hagar continued speaking. "Where is the thumb drive you promised me?"

The assistant was smart enough not to look the madman in the eyes. He kept his attention glued to the ground. "I don't know. He must have taken it. I've checked everywhere, and it's gone."

"Who's he?" Meg whispered. "The chief?"

"That's unfortunate for you." The terrorist paced around the man in an ever-tightening circle, his combat boots smashing the debris on the tiles. He stuck his hands in the pockets of his jacket, pretending to be deep in thought. "We had a deal, and you have not held up your end."

"I can't hand over something I don't have," Anderson said. "He shouldn't have had access to the safe, but somehow, he managed to break into it and steal your information."

Hagar's circle grew smaller, one boot smacking the back of Anderson's shoe as he passed. "Why do I not believe you?"

Anderson's shoulders slumped. "It's the truth. Your man already checked me over. I don't have the drive, and I've searched everywhere. He didn't hide it here."

Hagar stopped before him, leaning over to put his face in front of Anderson's. "Surely, the information is still on his computer. You can access that, yes?"

Anderson started to reply, then stopped himself, as if thinking it over. "Maybe. If I can get his password..."

Declan's internal bullshit meter went haywire. Anderson was playing with fire... Whoever put the information on that USB did it for a reason, and most likely, to get it off a work computer. Or it had never been there to begin with.

Why did Hagar want it?

Whatever the reason, Anderson was buying time, and Declan had to respect the man for it. Unfortunately, he feared Marchetti's assistant was almost out of time.

And if Declan was reading the look in Meg's eyes, she thought the same.

"We need a distraction," she whispered. "We have to save him."

Hagar gestured at his lieutenant, who grabbed the man by the shoulder and jerked him to his feet. "Where is his office?"

Anderson stumbled slightly. "Second floor. "

The terrorist leader made a sweeping gesture with his hand. "Take me there."

They started walking directly toward Declan and Meg.

She grabbed Dec and hustled him toward the nearest door, labeled as a meeting room. He took her arm and dragged her toward the stairwell instead. "He made us— you. We have to get out of here."

She protested, but he tightened his hold, forcing her to keep up.

"The supply closet," she hissed.

That was lengths of hallways and corridors away. This place was a maze. "No time."

He hit the bar on the fire door, shoving it open and flinging her onto the landing. "Up," he ordered as he forced the door shut behind them.

Before it clicked shut, he heard them enter the hall. As anticipated, they opened every door along the way.

Meg was already climbing, taking the steps two at a time.

He barreled after her, then passed her. She couldn't keep up with his strides, twice as long as hers. Reaching back, he offered her a hand, and she took it, but even when he tugged her along, it wasn't fast enough.

The door below opened. Declan hefted her over his shoulder and raced as quietly as he could up the next flight.

Below, men filed into the landing and started the climb.

He froze, but only for an instant. There were four of Hagar's men, Anderson, and Hagar himself. The amount of shuffling, talking, and general clamor they made was enough to drown out his footsteps.

So he ran.

Bypassing the second-floor entrance.

Up to the third-floor landing.

Controlling his breathing, he kept going.

Pounding feet echoed on the stairs beneath them, then stopped. Hagar barked an order in Farsi. *Search for stragglers.*

One of the group broke away.

And started up as Hagar and the rest entered the second floor.

Meg smacked him on the shoulder to put her down.

At war with himself, he allowed her body to slide down his chest until her feet touched the concrete floor of the small, square landing.

But he didn't let go.

As the death squad member whistled and jogged up the next set of steps, Declan grabbed his gun from Meg's waistband. Meg brought up her handheld ultrasonic weapon.

They moved as one into the shadows in the tight corner, each ready to take out their pursuer should he discover them.

A cell phone went off, ringing loud in the cavernous space. The man stopped and answered. He must have lowered himself to one of the steps because they heard the clatter of his weapon as it caught on the railing. He rattled off a conversation in his native language, and Declan pulled Meg from their hiding spot. He motioned her to continue up as he covered her backside, his gun pointed toward Hagar's man.

When they hit the next floor, she eased open the fire door, and they slipped inside.

This level was private quarters. None of the residents who called the place home, however, were here.

Meg stopped him before he could lead her away from the door. "We have to stop this," she said, her voice barely audible.

The hallway here was intact and homey-looking, like an old-fashioned hotel. Fancy fixtures, ornate antiques, and expensive paintings lined the space. It was as if the carnage below hadn't affected it at all.

Declan rubbed his temples. "This Anderson guy is an idiot and working with Hagar. Wonder who the man is that he said stole the USB? Tommy? Whose office is he taking Hagar to? His?"

"We should follow and find out. Hagar didn't make us. He saw me peeking at him and realized there were state employees on the loose, that's all. That's why he sent his man after stragglers."

"You understood that?"

"Yes."

Chasing after Hagar and Anderson would be stupid but might yield the answers they needed. Still... "Our orders are to evacuate."

"That was before we knew about our mystery man taking the USB and the fact that the intel might still be on his computer."

"We should report in and let Flynn decide what he wants us to do."

"We should." She gave him an evil grin. "But all I'm getting is static, which means we're on our own."

The unspoken words—*it's my call*—hung in the air between them. She was the team leader. He was her second. His role was set in stone.

And his earlier admission? He would pay for that at some point. Maybe now. "Are you asking me to disobey a direct order, not only from our boss but from the Deputy Director of the CIA?"

"Stone gave you the order to protect me at all costs?"

Michael Stone walked on water in Declan's book. He would go to hell and back for the man. "The one and only."

"Following me back down to the second floor and helping me figure out what happened to the USB isn't defying him, though. You'd actually be following his orders, wouldn't you?"

"You're asking me to walk a fine line. We both know that pursuing the USB will put you in imminent danger."

"I'm a black swan. Every mission puts me in imminent danger."

That truth couldn't be disputed. Nor could the fact that every mission went sideways, no matter how well-prepped they were.

Flynn had thrown them into this disaster without any warning. While he trusted them to figure things out on the fly to solve their own troublesome situations, ordering them to bail seemed like a copout. Was he trying to cover his ass, which was caught in a sling between the president —who'd demanded he activate their tiny, damaged division—and a no-win situation?

Declan gravitated to no-win situations. They made his pulse quicken and his blood heat.

Meg was one of them. A no-win relationship that he was bound and determined to turn around.

Win-win.

That was his goal.

At that moment, the director's voice startled them both. "What are you still doing there?" Flynn demanded through their comms. "The Romanian police have called in their SWAT team. Do not get caught. Evacuate now!"

Meg lifted her brows a fraction in question. Declan sighed and gave a nod. "I follow you," he said softly.

Meg's grin broadened. She made some static noises in her throat, totally unbelievable. "Sorry, you're breaking up, sir. What was"—more fake static—"...can't...hear..." Static. "...you..."

She removed the earbud, sliding it into her pocket.

Everything in his past came down to this moment. Was he really about to throw it all away? Because sure as shit, if he did this, he would never work for the CIA again. He'd be blacklisted. Hell, he'd probably end up in a black site prison, and no one would ever hear from him again.

The thrill of it charged the blood in his veins. That, and the open invitation on Meg's face. *Follow me into hell.*

Stone would have to move over.

He removed his comm, hearing the distant sound of Flynn's voice yelling at them, and turned it off. "If you want my help, let me take the lead," he challenged.

Her grin faded. "Blackmail? Seriously?"

"Seriously, *sunshine.*" He tweaked the end of her nose again, which he knew she hated as much as Spence's too-cheerful British slang. "Do we have a deal?"

If steam could've come out of her ears, it would have. Her lips pressed into an irritated, straight line, and she stepped away from the door, hands on her hips again. "Fine. What's our next move, oh great and wise Declan Reid?"

ELEVEN

The grin Dec shot her made her blood boil, but she couldn't help the racing of her heart at the sight of it. She'd missed that wicked look. The one that suggested he was about to lead her into something dangerous and heroic.

"Every embassy has a communications director who handles tech support. Regardless of what Anderson said, if we can find our tech in the group downstairs, we can get access to that information before Hagar."

It was a reasonable plan of action, but Hagar and Anderson were already three steps ahead of them. There might not be enough time to get to the gymnasium, find the person they needed, and do what had to be done. "Remember Sarajevo?" Meg asked.

"Which time?"

"The four bomb special."

The grin left his face, and she was sorry about that. "What about it?"

"We need to do the same thing here."

"This is a completely different situation."

"Is it?" That night, the president had been attending a private party at an estate that only a handful of people were to know about. It was a secret meeting of potential allies. The swans had been nearby after shutting down a potential health epidemic. The CIA had learned that the estate was about to be blown sky-high, and evacuating it would alert authorities and the press. The swans were to get in, defuse the bombs, and get out without anyone being the wiser. "We have hostages, a wanted terrorist, a missing person, and top-secret information that needs to be retrieved. Four bombs, four of us."

"Hate to remind you of this, but Tessa is not one of us."

"She would argue that I bet. While she might not have been on previous missions with us and understand our protocols to the letter, she survived plenty of assignments during her tenure as an operative that went Ringley Brothers on her." It was a term they'd coined for a situation that had dissolved into a circus. "She can help us handle this."

"Divide and conquer," he muttered.

"Our mission was to retrieve the USB, but I can't in good conscience leave those hostages behind or let Hagar go free. We have to stop him from getting that information at whatever cost, and beyond all of that, we need to find Tommy."

He paced a few feet away, thinking it over. Came

back, his expression grim. "Dividing us up like that is too dangerous."

"It's the only way," she argued.

He did the pacing thing again. She realized she'd missed that. He always thought better when he was moving. "We bring in Spence and Tessa to handle the hostages. You and I go after the intel and Hagar."

Her blood boiled again. "That's an efficient use of our resources."

He tugged out his earbud. "On the contrary, that's the best use of them. I know what you're thinking, Meg. You were going to put yourself in charge of going after Hagar. Do you really think I'd go along with that?"

No, she didn't, but she'd had to give it a try. "I want to look in his eyes when I kill him. For Jessie."

"A quick death is too easy. I figured you'd want to turn him over to Flynn."

"I don't trust myself to do that." She pointed at her temple. "I'm...messed up. I might..."

"Torture him first?"

She'd considered it.

Dec knew she had and didn't judge her for it. "Anyone who went through what you did with Hagar would be messed up. They would want to see him suffer in retaliation for what he did to Jessie. Nothing you do to help yourself will work until he's paid for what he did, and it's by your hand. Stop beating yourself up over it."

She sucked in a breath. *Nothing you do...*

Damn it. He was right.

Again.

She'd been spinning her wheels, trying everything under the sun to find a way to come to terms with it. To make herself suffer over and over in recompense.

But it wasn't enough. Would never be enough.

So, here she was, still mired in that bastard's manipulative and cruel filth. Hagar was nothing but rotting scum, and he'd pulled her down into it. Drowned her in it.

She wanted revenge. She wanted him to suffer. He was a sadist who had hurt so, so many people.

He should be dead, not Jessie.

"You're not a damn saint, Meg." Declan was still reading her mind. Still absolving her from wanting to take all her hurt and rage out on Hagar in a very un-Meg-like way. Brutal. Vicious. Remorseless.

That was her fantasy. One of them, anyway.

Being on this mission, though, had taken the edge off her hopelessness. Being with Dec and Spence again. Using her skills and cunning to recruit Tessa. Even following—and then bucking—Flynn's orders.

It had all reminded her of what she'd once loved. This work wasn't for most folks, but for her? She was a natural at handling turmoil and upheaval.

She touched the pendant, feeling Jessie's steadying presence. "When I catch up with Hagar, I'll make it quick and clean, but I'll be sure to record his execution at my hands to allow the world to witness his final breaths, just like he put Jessie's death on display. And yeah, I know. Vigilante justice will be a one-way ticket off the swans and into prison. I don't care."

He nodded as if he'd do exactly the same thing. "For the record, it won't bring you peace, but it will bring a certain level of satisfaction."

"Don't assume you know what will bring me peace."

He raised his hands in surrender. "Fair enough."

She didn't need peace. She needed to be able to look Tommy in the eye and know she'd done what she could to honor Jessie's memory. "I didn't mean that to come out so..."

"Pissed?" He chuckled, rubbing a hand up and down her arm in a soothing gesture. "It's okay. I'm used to it."

She punched his bicep. Hard as a rock, like always.

He stuck the earbud back in his ear. "Swans Three and Four, we require your assistance. There are a number of embassy employees trapped in the building's gymnasium on the ground floor. Figure out a plan to get them out safely and enact it. You have five minutes."

His face scrunched, and she knew Flynn had commandeered the airwaves. She stuck in her own earbud and switched it on in time to hear the director's voice, "...incoming SWAT team breach. Your orders are to abort and evacuate."

The thing was, he wasn't yelling. His voice was deadly calm and pitched low enough to make the hair on her arms stand up.

"The moment the police arrive, sir, those folks become hostages for Hagar," Dec said. "We can prevent that."

Meg held her breath. The swans were never to go off mission. Were never to be publicly noticed or hailed as heroes. They were shadows, ghosts. Performing a humanitarian feat like this was outside the parameters and scope of their operations. What she was asking—what Dec was ordering Spence and Tessa to do—would get them all fired.

So be it. She was already walking that tightrope and hadn't wanted to be activated to begin with.

She once again removed her earbud, unwilling to listen to Dec and Flynn argue. Instead, she roamed the chief of mission's personal quarters, noting the normality of it. The suite wasn't opulent, but it was nicer than any place she'd ever lived.

After her quick walk-through, she rejoined Dec in time to hear him say, "...with all due respect, sir, you're not in our shoes at the moment. You threw us all here, and we can't fulfill the mission to recover the USB because it isn't where it was supposed to be. The Black Swan Division can handle this turn of events and will do so under the guidance of our leader. Swan One has a plan, and we will follow it. I believe it was JFK who said, 'In a crisis, be aware of the danger, but recognize the opportunity.' That's what we're doing. Black Swan Two over and out."

She blinked as he gruffly jammed the comm in his cargo pants. "You just signed your termination papers."

He shrugged and opened the door. "Let's go get us a terrorist."

TWELVE

Worst. Decision. Ever.

Declan moved silently beside Meg as they crept through the dimly lit office corridor. They avoided the guard in the stairwell by using the Chief of Mission's private elevator to get down to the second floor.

The air was thick with tension, every step calculated, and each one of their breaths measured. The rioters outside had not dispersed and now had set up metal barrels that flickered with fires, radios playing music at loud decibels, and shouts and laughter. It was a party.

So far, the SWAT team had made no appearance. Neither had any US military force. Declan couldn't decide whether that was good or bad.

In here, the quiet was unnerving, broken only by the faint hum of electronics and the partying going on outside.

Whoever had the USB was playing a game, and it didn't sit right with him. His gut told him something worse was about to unfold. He'd lost count of the many surprises they'd already encountered.

Megan nudged him, pointing at the rear entrance to what was considered the bullpen of the embassy—a sprawling office filled with cubicles. This was where most of the grunt work behind the public access areas went on.

He raised a hand to stop her, and the two of them squatted and peered over the ledge of one of the large glass windows that revealed the cubicles. Like in the other areas of the building, this one had been evacuated in a panic. Most of the waist-high dividers still stood, but some of the chairs had been tipped over, personal effects left behind on desks, and a variety of debris littered the floor.

The main door and matching set of windows were opposite them. The cubicle walls were a soft, blue fabric, and the closest one had pictures of kids pinned to a spot above the desk. Some school pictures, others of a family in various poses. Birthdays, Christmases, beach vacations. There was a framed photo of a couple in their wedding attire sitting next to a mug that read World's Best Mom.

Had the woman escaped, or was she one of those in the gymnasium, hoping for a rescue?

He wanted to open up the comms and check with Spence and Tessa about progress on that end, but didn't want to risk distracting them.

Or have another fight with Flynn.

Meg nudged him again, pointing at a group man with his back to them at one of the farthest cubicles.

Hagar.

Three squad members hung out near the main entrance to the bullpen, one of them pacing in front of the windows. Another occasionally glanced over his shoulder toward the rear set of windows they crouched under. Confident no one would impede their plan, he seemed unconcerned about unwelcome visitors.

That allowed Declan and Meg to keep their presence unknown while studying them and figuring out their best move.

Declan's concentration was divided, however. He needed to assess the situation and make a plan, but part of him knew Meg needed to take the lead. Exacting vengeance—or justice, whichever term she preferred— would do her more good than hours of therapy or any of that other bullshit psychology stuff the CIA wanted to force on her.

He'd been in the trenches too many times, saw too many guys have their power stripped away, and could never regain it. A few who managed some form of retribution usually slept better at night. Not all, but some. When you'd seen the atrocities committed by criminals and terrorists, handing them their ass gave you more satisfaction than any other thing he could think of.

Hagar held a gun pressed to Anderson's head, his demeanor calm and unflinching as Anderson typed frantically. The man had bought himself some time by claiming he could bypass the computer security protocols and access the needed files, but as he continued to work, Dec knew he'd lied. He was no computer whiz, and he certainly didn't have the skills to hack into anyone else's files.

As the bored minion made a circuit past them, Dec and Meg ducked, hiding under his line of sight. They listened intently for him to move on. Their eyes locked, and Dec searched hers for any sign that she was about to come unglued. She had to be holding herself together by a thread, knowing Hagar was only a few yards away, and he wished he could make this easier for her.

She gave him a tremulous smile as if seeing his thoughts visible on his face. He'd rarely been able to hide his from her. They'd always been in sync, no words needed between them.

A gun went off, and she recoiled. He started to lurch upward to see what had happened, but the sheer panic on her face stopped him.

Had Hagar shot Anderson?

He grabbed Meg's hand and squeezed it hard. She blinked.

Her shoulders dropped, and releasing a soft breath, she nodded, reassuring him she was okay.

Was she?

Slowly, he eased up to peer into the room. Anderson had covered his head with his hands, and Hagar was lowering his gun from where he'd put a bullet in the ceiling rather than the man's head.

As if that might encourage the man to work more efficiently.

Idiot. All he'd done was make Anderson crap his pants. As Hagar smacked him on the back of his head, he said, "Quit sniffling and do what I told you to." He looked at his watch. "You have thirty seconds."

The man was shaking so hard now that he couldn't even type. Meg slid up to peer in at the scene.

He knew she was torn—should they save Anderson? The only way to do so would be to take out Hagar and his goons. Could they access the computer and find the intel they'd come for?

Dec started to tug her back down to tell her what he thought when the guard at the front door went on high alert. "He's here."

Hagar and Anderson's heads snapped toward the entrance, and Dec's stomach dropped to his knees.

Seeing who had joined the party, Meg sucked in an audible breath, her fingers gripping the ledge. "What the…?"

Tommy Mendoza stepped into the room. His hair was longer than the last time Declan had seen him, and he'd pulled it back into one of those stupid man buns. He'd put on some weight, too, and a beard outlined his jaw.

Gone was the young man so full of eagerness to serve his country, and in its place was a seasoned soldier. "Heard you were looking for me," he said, sticking out his chest in a show of bravado.

Hagar's face brightened. "Mendoza, come, come." He held out his hand. "You owe me something, I believe."

The guard used his gun to push Tommy forward.

"Tommy," Meg whispered under her breath, her disbelief echoing Declan's own.

The boy didn't seem panicked. In fact, he looked almost...pleased. As if he'd planned this all along.

Surprise number...? Right, he'd forgotten to keep track.

Declan's jaw tightened as Tommy held up a small object between his fingers. "Did you think I would renege on our deal?"

"You didn't show up at the designated meeting spot," Hagar said. "What was I supposed to think?"

The USB. In his gut, Declan had no doubt that's what the kid held outstretched between him and the terrorist.

Was Tommy a traitor? Was this leverage of some kind? Had he lost his fucking mind?

Hagar started to swipe the drive from his fingers, but the young man snatched it back. "No need to waste time with my computer," Tommy said to Anderson. "I wouldn't leave highly classified information on there, anyway." He jutted his chin toward Anderson as he met Hagar's rueful smile. "He's not part of this. Let him go."

Meg whispered in Declan's ear, "We can't let that USB fall into Hagar's hands." She swallowed hard, her eyes on Tommy the way a mother would look at a son. "And we have to save Tommy. Hagar will kill him."

She reached for the ultrasonic weapon and pulled out the earplugs. The weapon would incapacitate those inside for a couple of minutes, and that might be all they needed.

But then she dropped her hand from it. "Tommy's in the line of fire."

Which would make him a challenge to move if he was unable to walk on his own. It was risky—a blunt solution for a situation this delicate—but what choice did they have? They couldn't shoot all the terrorists, save Tommy, and grab the USB.

Before Declan could insist she go with her gut and use it, footsteps thundered behind them, followed by the unmistakable click of a gun safety being disengaged.

He whipped around in time to see the trigger-happy suit who'd fired on Meg earlier. God, it seemed like a lifetime ago already.

He'd only left the man unconscious, and now, his good deed had backfired. The hidden doorway the suit had emerged from was still cracked open. Apparently, the chief of mission not only had a private elevator but also a private staircase.

The guy narrowed his eyes at Meg. "You."

She raised the hand with the earplugs as if in surrender, but Declan saw the device in her other next to her side, ready to fire. "Yes, me," she said quietly. "There's a hostage situation in there." She pointed at the bullpen. "I need you to turn around and go back where you came from. We're handling it."

His attention darted toward the windows, and he started to lower his weapon, but then his gaze flicked back to her and snagged on her half-hidden weapon that looked exactly like a handgun. Without hesitation, he raised his gun and...

Declan tackled Meg as he saw the man's finger squeeze the trigger.

The shot cracked through the air, whizzing past Declan's head as he slammed Meg to the floor. The bullet pinged off the elevator door, and shouts erupted inside the bullpen.

No need for quiet or stealth now. In one swift movement, he palmed his sidearm and shot the man in the knee.

The guard screamed and fell to the ground, gripping his leg and cursing. His weapon hit the ground and spun a few feet away.

Meg leaped to her feet, retrieving the weapon and pocketing it. Next, she snatched up the fallen earplugs and stuck them in her ear. I warned you," she grumbled, staring down at him. "Wrap your tie around it to stop the bleeding. You'll be fine."

"He fucking shot me!" the man yelled.

Declan gestured for her to get down again as he chanced a glance into the bullpen. Hagar had spun toward them, gun raised, finger on the trigger. Anderson had scrambled for cover and was nowhere to be seen. Tommy just stood there, frozen.

Stupid kid.

Not a kid, he told himself. But still an idiot for all his swagger and fake confidence.

Hagar's goons rushed for them, AK-15s aimed at the windows. Declan ducked and waved Meg toward the stairs. "Abort!"

"No," she said and grabbed the handle of the door.

He knew what she was about to do, and he cursed under his breath but raised his gun and fell into step right behind her, bringing it up under her raised arm as he rested a hand on her waist.

It was a move they had perfected in Switzerland three years ago, and he still loved its beauty, its simplicity.

In sync once more, she launched herself through the door.

THIRTEEN

She fired.

Dec fired.

The men with the semi-automatics went down first. Dec had nailed two of them, her weapon had sent the other two curling into fetal positions.

Hagar grunted, staggering back and grabbing his head. His gun slipped from his fingers.

Tommy's knees buckled, the USB falling from his grasp as he collapsed, disoriented but still conscious.

Anderson groaned from underneath his desk.

Neither of them wasted a second. Declan surged across the room to retrieve the weapons, and she was glad the ultrasonic weapon hadn't affected him at all. She yanked out her earplugs and snatched up the USB. For the span of a heartbeat, relief flooded through her. "Got it."

Finally.

Tommy whimpered at her feet. What was she going

to do with him? She leaned down and shook him, her fingers digging into his shoulder. "Tommy, what are you doing here?"

He blinked up at her, and she didn't know if it was because he didn't recognize her or simply wasn't expecting her to be there. Either way, all he did was moan, still reeling from the blast.

She tried to force him into a seated position, but he kept falling over. Declan would have to carry him out.

She turned to tell him so and heard him yell, "Watch your six!"

In her peripheral vision, a shadow lunged for her. Hagar.

He was off balance but managed to grab her by the hair and yank. It pulled her backward, off balance.

Instinct, combined with years of self-defense training, had her twist to face him. Ignoring the pain of her hair being pulled from her scalp, she kicked his shin to destabilize him.

He roared with rage, falling, but didn't release her, his weight pulling her down with him.

He rolled, pinning her under him, and—too late—she saw him reach for his fallen handgun.

She tried to jam her thumbs into his eyeballs. He jerked his head from side to side, avoiding her probing fingers. Changing tactics, she boxed his ears.

Declan loomed above them, seizing the terrorist by the back of his jacket and yanking him off of her. He tossed him aside as if he were an old shirt rather than a two-hundred-pound man.

Meg snatched up Hagar's gun as Dec pulled her to her feet. Anderson reached out from under the desk and grabbed her ankle. "Help me," he said, his words slurred as if he were drunk.

She yanked him out of his hiding place and shoved him toward the exit. "Go!" She would deal with him later. He started crawling for the door.

The squad members who'd been closest to the ultrasonic weapon when it went off were still down for the count, but the two who'd been behind Tommy were recovering. One staggered to his feet, going for the pile of weapons Declan had made. Dec popped the guy on the temple with the butt of his gun. The man went down, a solid KO.

Hagar got to his hands and knees, eyes locked on Meg again. His sadistic gaze raked over her, and it was all she could do not to kick him in the face. "You are one tough bastard," she told him, "but you're done. It's over. You're coming with us to be tried in a court of law for your crimes against humanity."

Dec blinked in surprise but didn't argue, and she hoped one of the security guards had handcuffs. She wasn't sure how she was going to march Hagar out and get him back to the States, but dammit, she *was* going to see justice done.

Either that, or she was going to put a bullet in his brain and not look back.

I'm not that person, she told herself, even though there was a very cold, desolate part of her that claimed differently. A devil on her shoulder, whispering for her to

do it right now. To take Dec's gun and end it, making sure
Hagar never terrorized anyone again.

Jessie, her sister of the heart. Her teammate.

She rubbed the pendant, sending up that familiar
prayer. The old agony clawed at her heart, shredding it
all over again, but at least this time, there might be a sliver
of peace in sight.

As if Hagar knew where her thoughts had gone, he
smirked. "I will haunt you forever. She will, too. Her
death is on you."

Dec drew out a pair of flexicuffs and jerked first one
and then the other of Hagar's arms behind him. "Yeah,
yeah. We all know you're a douchebag, and you love to
terrorize people. As you can see, Meg is fully recovered,
and she just kicked your ass. Now,"—she jerked the man
to his feet—"get up."

The terrorist struggled against Dec's strength and the
restraints, but Declan was a force to be reckoned with.
Meg glanced toward the open door, hearing the shouts of
the SWAT team finally arriving. She wasn't sure how to
convince them that she and Declan were the good guys,
but then she saw Tessa leading the charge down the hall.

Meg let go of a soft laugh.

And then she realized Anderson wasn't the only one
who had managed to escape.

Panic flooded through her. "Dec, where's Tommy?"

Her second turned, scanning the room with her.

Tessa and the SWAT team barreled in. Her eyes
landed on Hagar, and she smiled. "Look what the swans
bagged today."

"Did you see Tommy?" Meg asked.

"Tommy?" Tessa shook her head. "He was here?"

The SWAT team leader ordered his men to lower their weapons. Then he demanded an explanation in broken English, but Meg shoved past him, trying to reach the door. "I have to find him."

Armored officers blocked her way. None of them would let her pass, their leader demanding an explanation again.

"I told you what you need to know," Tessa complained to the brute of a man who towered over all of them. She said something in Romanian, possibly repeating herself in his language. "Mosai Hagar is a wanted terrorist that we've captured. We'll escort him to the 71st Airbase, where a team will be waiting to take him to the United States."

The SWAT team leader responded in Romanian, and Meg felt her insides twist. She couldn't translate his words, but she knew by the way he dismissed Hagar with barely a glance that something was amiss. Tessa's face fell, and she started arguing with him.

Hagar gave Meg a satisfied smile.

The SWAT team leader gestured at him and the flexicuffs, then at one of his men, who stepped forward. Dec pulled Hagar back, keeping away from the eager officer. He raised his gun. "Over your dead body."

The man stopped, glancing at his commander. Tessa did some fast talking in Romanian, propelling Meg through the blockage of black-clad SWAT members. "Go after Tommy, I'll handle this."

Meg considered her options. She had the USB. She would alert Flynn to let him know that Hagar was about to walk away. Flynn would do something.

He had to. She couldn't let Hagar get away again.

Should've put a bullet in the bastard's head.

She holstered her weapon, raising her hands in surrender as she pushed past the SWAT officers. Declan held his ground, giving her a nod when she glanced at him. He winked. "Go get our boy," he said.

She gave Hagar a pointed look. "Even if you walk free today," she told him, "you better keep looking over your shoulder. I'm a ghost, and I'll haunt you forever."

She squeezed through the line of officers and, once free, ran for the stairwell. Tommy couldn't have gotten far with the lasting effects of the ultrasonic blast slowing him down. She was going to find him.

And when she did?

She was going to kick his ass.

FOURTEEN

Damn it. Declan stood in the middle of the embassy courtyard, swearing a blue streak. He'd had to turn over Hagar to the Romanian police, and the bastard now slumped against the concrete wall, his defiant glare fixed on Declan.

The SWAT team leader had listened to Tessa's insistent pleas that they not turn the man loose. That he was the instigator behind the riots, but Declan knew something was going on behind the scenes. If anything, the police seemed blasé about the whole thing. Annoyed that they had to deal with the situation. Unconcerned that they had one of the most wanted terrorists in the world in their possession.

He wouldn't be surprised if Hagar were on the loose again before morning.

Adrenaline burned through him, partly from the takedown and partly from watching Meg run out the door. Keeping one eye on Hagar, he made his way through the gathered crowd, some of them injured and being treated by emergency responders. Others still partying.

No Meg. No Tommy.

Shit.

He caught sight of Spence, who waved a hand over the heads of a mixed group of men and women dressed in suits. Embassy employees. He tugged someone with him as he skirted around them—a dark-haired woman covered in dirt and stains.

Meg.

As Declan breathed a quiet sigh of relief, she raised her hands. "I lost him."

"*We* lost him," Spence corrected. "I was helping the hostages out of the building at the rear dock when Tommy came barreling through. I didn't recognize him. Meg told me what happened upstairs. I can't believe he's in cahoots with that wanker."

Declan couldn't believe it himself. "Did you see which way he went?"

One of the embassy employees sought out Spence to praise him for his assistance. He assured her it was no problem and directed her toward a woman with a medical vest on who was carrying a blanket.

Once she was out of hearing, he turned back to Declan and Meg. "He went south. I thought he was heading for the Metro, but by the time I realized it was him, he was blocks away. I trailed him until he jumped into a waiting taxi."

"Tell me you can identify it," Declan said.

"Of course." Spence pointed at his earbud. "You better check in. Solomon is having a cow. I'll dig up the number of the ride company, but it's after hours. We may not be able to get any information until morning."

A rumble of engines cut through the night air, and a line of black vehicles rolled up, sleek and imposing. There were no markings on the sides to identify them as Romanian or American, but the group that piled out in unmarked uniforms told Declan they were military.

They cut through the crowd, the lead operative confronting the Romanian SWAT team leader. "We're taking custody of the prisoners."

"Who are they?" Meg asked, getting pushed by the crush of people around them trying to evade the newcomers.

"You stay here with Spence," Declan said. "I'll handle this."

She wasn't about to listen to him. Imagine that. She took hold of the back of his jacket, trailing behind him. "We can't let Hagar get away."

He knew that, and yet... concessions would have to be made. It was something he hated more than anything, but they were still in the same position. Hagar graced plenty of Wanted posters in countries other than the States, and although plenty were after him for his crimes, he had friends and allies and high places, including the governments of many of those countries.

By the time the two of them reached the SWAT team leader and his military counterpart, the two men were in each other's faces arguing. Hagar and his men were being jerked up from their seats on the ground and lined up against the wall. Hagar didn't resist, but his eyes never left Declan's. In those cold, depthless orbs, he was letting him know it wasn't over yet.

Tessa emerged from the front of the destroyed building, stepping over the debris and hailing them. "Time for us to go," she called, making shooing motions with her hands.

By the time she reached them, the argument had escalated into a yelling match that was gaining the attention of all of those on the grounds. She grabbed both Declan and Meg, pushing them with the strength of someone twice her size and marching them towards Spence. "We are not supposed to be here," she said over the crowd noise and the arguing men. "And if we don't leave now, we may find ourselves behind bars, right along with Hagar."

Meg started to argue, but Declan grabbed her arm, and along with Tessa, they escorted her toward the destroyed gates, Spence falling into stride with them.

Once they were clear of the commotion, Declan forced all of them into a bus stop shelter near the spot where Spence claimed to have seen Tommy disappear into the taxi. It had to be nearing midnight, and the buses had stopped running hours ago.

"We have the drive," Declan said, watching Meg stare into the distance. He knew what she was thinking. Could tell by the way she shook out her hands and paced that she was full of pent-up energy. The adrenaline hadn't yet worn off, and now she had a new mission—

Tommy. "The red bag mission is finished. We take the USB, and we meet Pegasus at the designated spot."

Meg's eyes flashed with irritation. "We're *not* done. Tommy's out there, and he's caught up in some kind of mess. If he's working with Hagar—"

"We don't know that," Declan interrupted, his voice low but firm.

"What if he's the reason all of this happened in the first place?" Her eyes lost the snapping anger, and her voice lowered to meet his. "What if he's after his own version of revenge for Jessie's death?"

It was the only scenario she could spin that would make Tommy a hero. The alternatives were too painful for her to consider. "I know you want to think the best of him—I do, too—but he made a deal with Hagar to hand over the USB."

She dropped her head into her hands. "I know. It was all too calculated. To premeditated." She pulled out the drive and turned it over in her fingers. "What the hell is on here that would tempt Hagar enough to create a riot in order to retrieve it? He's a showman, that's for sure, but that little display back there"—she hitched a thumb over her shoulder toward the embassy—"isn't his style. Too risky."

Declan nodded. "The whole thing stinks, but right now, getting the USB to Flynn is our only priority. We'll figure out the rest later."

"You go, then," Meg said, her tone now clipped. "You and Spence meet Pegasus at the rendezvous point. Tessa and I will find Tommy."

In a show of solidarity, Tessa sidled closer to Meg, lifting her chin.

Declan glared at them, his chest tight. "Spence can take the USB. I'm not leaving you."

"Wait just a bloody minute." Spence's hands fisted. "I thought we were a team. If you're hunting Tommy, then we're all hunting him."

Meg shoved the USB at him and gave him a look that brooked no argument. "We *are* a team, but right now, we have a dual mission that requires us to use our assets wisely. Take this and meet Pegasus. On the way, if you happen to break through the encryption and figure out what's on it, you might accidentally let it slip to me, so I have leverage with Tommy when I find him."

Spence started to argue but closed his mouth and gave a resigned shake of his head. "Fine. But you better smack him upside the head for me when you do." He yanked out his phone, his fingers moving rapidly over the screen. "Here's the number for the taxi company and the car's tag number."

"We *will* find him," Meg replied, her eyes scanning the dark streets. "Now go. Be safe."

She wasn't a hugger, but Spence grabbed her and held her to him, murmuring something in her ear too low for Declan to hear. She patted his back, and Tessa squeezed his arm as he turned to leave.

"I want the record to show that I'm against splitting up," he said to Declan, even as he stepped outside the shelter.

"Noted," Declan said. "Thanks, man."

Spence drew a cloth bag from one of his pockets and shoved it into Declan's hand. "These are set for a different frequency than our current comms. The four of us can stay in contact without Langley listening in." He gave each of them a pointed look. "As soon as you can, get them up and running so I know what's going on, understand?"

It was a rare thing for Spence to hand out orders. Meg gave him a thumbs-up. "We will."

As she hurried away, Meg called the taxi company. The woman spoke in Romanian, and she put her on speakerphone so Tessa could communicate with her. Declan had to hand it to Meg—adding The Architect to their group had been a wise decision.

Unfortunately, Spence was right. Since it was after hours, all the clerk on the phone could do was help them set up a ride. She couldn't offer any information about the taxi that had picked up Tommy. She suggested calling back after eight a.m. and speaking to one of the owners.

"Tell her it's an emergency," Meg assisted.

Apparently, the operator did speak some English.

"I cannot give out the information. You will have to call back."

She disconnected. Meg cursed under her breath and jammed the phone into her pocket. "What now?"

"Now we wait," Tessa said. The setback was no big deal in her eyes. "I have a place not far from here. You two could use a shower and some rest." She waved her fingers under her nose, letting them know they smelled offensive. "The pantry is fully stocked, and the closets have clean clothes." This time, she gave them an assessing once-over. "You can't go around looking like that without calling attention to yourself."

Meg looked down at her clothes and winced when she smelled her armpits. "You're right, but..."

"No buts," Tessa said.

Declan held in his smirk at the annoyance that tightened Meg's face. "Funny," he said, "sounds like you have a safe house in Bucharest. I thought you got out of the spy game."

Tessa gave him a charming smile. "No one ever gets out of the spy game, Dec. You know that."

Meg rolled her eyes. "I see you've already conveniently forgotten our conversation in the library yesterday."

Tessa glanced at her watch. "Technically, that was two days ago." She headed out of the shelter. "Try to keep up."

Meg shot Declan a look that suggested she wanted to revoke Tessa's membership in the Black Swan Division, but he just shrugged. "You're the one that recruited her."

She blew out a tired breath that lifted the bangs plastered to her forehead. "I don't want to sit around twiddling my thumbs."

"Neither do I, but she's right. We both look like shit, and neither of us has had food or so much as a nap in twenty-four hours. We're running on fumes, and this chase could last a while."

Tessa was halfway down the block, not bothering to look over her shoulder to see if they were following. Meg seemed to debate with herself. "We've been through worse, but this?" She shook her head. "I don't know Tommy well enough to say what he would or wouldn't do, but I always thought I could trust him, you know?"

He saw the disheartening sadness in her eyes. She didn't balk when he took her hand and drew her out of the bus stop shelter. The night sky was cloudy, but stars peeked out here and there. "We continue to trust him until we find proof otherwise."

Whether it was his touch or his words, he couldn't be sure, but she fell into step beside him, allowing her shoulder to bump his arm. She gave his hand a grateful squeeze. "We trust him until we find proof otherwise," she confirmed.

They walked in silence, leaving the chaos of the embassy far behind.

"Remember, Bruges?" he chanced to ask her.

She glanced up at the sky and smiled as if that romantic walk in Belgium was fresh in her mind. "How could I forget?"

That mission had ended with them sharing a bed. They'd had a whole weekend to themselves and stayed in a fancy hotel, rarely donning clothes except when room service brought their meals. Three days of sex, sleep, and talking.

Planning.

Planning for a future they both knew wasn't in the cards. A home, family, normal jobs...neither of them was cut out for that shit.

"Sometimes, I still think about it," he murmured,

linking an arm through hers and drawing her closer like a lover would do. "About those plans we made."

Her silence stretched out as they kept Tessa in sight, but she slowed their steps as if she wanted to draw out the moment a bit longer.

Finally, she leaned her head against his shoulder. "Sometimes, Dec," she said, barely above a whisper, "I do, too."

FIFTEEN

The safe house was a nondescript thing tucked away in a quiet corner of a rundown neighborhood outside the city.

The structure looked like any other old, weathered building in this part of town—a faded façade with crumbling bricks and shutters half open as if the house were afraid to see the world. Meg didn't blame it.

"Not much to look at," Declan muttered as they trudged up the overgrown sidewalk.

Morning was only a few hours away, and they had used a ride service to drop them off a few blocks south, but Meg's feet ached from all the walking—and running—she'd done in the past forty-eight hours. Her eyes would barely stay open.

Tessa glanced back at him. "Some might say the same about you."

Meg snorted, feeling punch-drunk. Dec shot her a look of consternation.

They entered through the rear, where Tessa punched

a code into the keyless lock. The wooden door creaked, and for a split second, Meg felt like she was entering a haunted house rather than a safe one.

Absolute darkness met her eyes before Tessa flicked on the lights. They hung their coats in the tiny mudroom, and Tessa reset the security system, rattling off the code for them to memorize.

The mudroom led to a kitchen with top-grade appliances. "There's an assortment of dry goods and canned foods in the pantry," Tessa said. "Frozen meals are in the freezer but I'm afraid it's light on perishables. I wasn't expecting company."

"Coffee?" Declan asked.

Tessa pointed to an upper cabinet before leading Meg through a small living room with a single bedroom and bath to the right.

One bedroom, one bed. Great.

Meg dropped onto the mattress, stretching out her aching shoulders. The tension that had built up in her body was impossible to shake. Her muscles screamed for rest, but her mind wouldn't let her. Not yet.

Declan surveyed each room with the sharp focus he always had on every mission, regardless of how tired he was. He checked the locks on the windows and front door and made sure all the blinds and curtains were closed.

Tessa caught Meg's eyes and rolled hers.

Meg found it comforting. Security systems could fail. Dec didn't.

"Towels and linens are in the bathroom closet," Tessa told them, walking back through the tiny place. "Clean clothes are in the armoire." She headed for the back door. "Let me know if you find Tommy."

Meg trailed after her, feeling a touch of panic at being alone with Declan. "Wait, you're leaving?"

Tessa glanced at the clock over the sink. "I have to be at work in four hours. Tell Flynn I'll send him a bill for my services." She waved. "It's been fun—kind of. Good luck."

As the door shut behind her, Meg stood in the mudroom, stunned. Declan reset the security system before brushing a hand over her back. "Why don't you go take a hot shower? I'll scrounge up some food."

She just stood there, everything crashing down on her like a giant wave in the ocean. Food and sleep would help, but then what? Tommy was out there somewhere in the night, and she couldn't stop thinking about what he'd done.

She didn't have all the facts, so jumping to conclusions was pointless, and yet...

Those conclusions pummeled her brain, regardless.

She hadn't realized he was employed at the embassy.

That he was the one with the information on that USB.

That Tommy—Jessie's baby brother—could even be in the same room with the man who had killed his sister and not seek revenge.

The idea that he might be working with him? That was too horrifying to entertain.

"Meg?"

She startled. Declan was staring at her.

He took her hand and let her toward the bathroom. "Come on."

He turned on the water, keeping his fingers under the stream until it warmed to his liking. It took a couple of tries to get the shower to work, but finally, it did.

He touched the lapel of her shirt, trailing one finger down the buttons. "Need help getting out of your clothes?"

His tone was sincere, but she saw the teasing in his eyes. She was grateful for it—his attempt at lightening the mood. She waved him off. "Still trying to get me naked," she retorted flippantly, pleased to see him smile.

"Holler if you need me to scrub your back," he offered as he walked out, shutting the door behind him.

The water pressure was weak, but it was warm, and that was better than she could hope for. She scrubbed herself from head to toe several times, letting some of her whirling thoughts go down the drain with the dirty water.

When she emerged, she found a set of folded clothes waiting on the sink for her. She was definitely distracted if she hadn't noticed him sneaking them in.

Of course, he'd always moved with silent and deadly precision. It shouldn't surprise her that he could get in and out without her noticing. Still, it annoyed her.

She was slipping.

Had slipped.

Would it ever stop?

Could she reverse it?

Leaving the bathroom, her nose led her to the

kitchen. He'd set places at the table and reheated a casserole that smelled heavenly.

"It was labeled chicken and mushroom," he told her. "Directions said to cook it in the oven, but I threw it in the microwave."

She sank into a chair and started shoveling the saucy noodles into her mouth. It wasn't the best she'd ever had, but it was damn good at the moment.

He sat across from her, but after a minute, she discovered he wasn't eating. He was simply staring at her.

"What?" she asked around a mouthful.

"Glad you haven't lost your appetite."

She shot him the finger and snagged a second helping. "You can take the couch for that comment."

"I already made it up."

She'd passed by it without noticing. Slipping, slipping, slipping... "What if we can't find him?" she blurted.

Dec dug into his food. "We will."

"What if we don't? He's young and inexperienced. He's caught up in something way over his head. I've seen enough to know how easy it is for someone like him to get messed up because they don't realize who they're messing with until it's too late."

"There's nothing you can do for him right now." He reached across the table and patted her hand. "We will find him, and no matter what he's got himself involved in, we'll help him get out of it."

Always so sure. One of the things she loved about him.

Had loved about him.

He'd been her rock through so many things and always seemed to be two steps ahead of her. His presence was welcome, and yet, it also complicated things. She couldn't ignore how her pulse kicked when he looked at her the way he was now. The way her heart skipped a beat when he touched her.

She should pull her hand away. Stop staring into those gorgeous eyes of his.

Instead, she set down her fork. She couldn't afford to have feelings for him, but here she was, drowning in them. "If I let my emotions cloud my judgment, it could jeopardize everything."

He knew she wasn't talking about Tommy. He laid down his fork as well, keeping a light hold of her hand. "Can you ever forgive me?"

She knew what he was asking.

She swallowed down the pit that lodged in her throat. *Projection*, her therapist had diagnosed. *Survivor's guilt.* Just a few of the terms the doctor had thrown at her.

"I never really blamed you." The words were like rough stones in her mouth. "I blamed myself, but you became my whipping post. I was consumed with guilt because she was my responsibility, and I failed her. Failed all of you. You became a target for me to take out all of my rage and self-loathing on." She was tired. So damn tired of it all. "I'm sorry. It wasn't fair."

"You know what I learned in the Marines?"

A lot of things, she bet. "How to properly curse?"

He smirked. "Besides that. I learned that the second in command is a sounding board for the commanding officer. In the war room, in the field, doesn't matter. The CO needs his second to be a wall. To bounce ideas off, to release pent-up frustration on, to rely on for support, no matter what the odds or situation. A real partner through thick and thin. Better or worse."

"You make it sound like a marriage."

"It is in a way." His thumb stroked over her fingers, one by one. Slow, soothing. "Whatever you can dish out, Meg, I can take it."

The way he looked at her sometimes, the moments like this when their interactions softened into casual banter... It was dangerous. "Do you ever..." She rolled her finger around her temple.

"Lose my shit? Who doesn't?"

"I've never seen you fall apart. Never seen you come undone like I have."

"I save it for the ring. I take out my frustrations through boxing." He glanced down at their connected hands. "You should try it sometime. Might do you some good. Probably more so than seeing that therapist."

"Hitting people isn't my thing."

"You can hit me. I can handle it. You won't hurt me."

She narrowed her eyes. "Is that so?"

He smirked. "I guarantee you hit like a girl."

Fat, rotten son of a bitch. "Sounds like you're throwing down a challenge."

"Take it however you want."

The tension in the air snapped like an electric wire between them. She wanted to take *him* right now. Sex—

fast, hard, knock-it-out-the-park skin-to-skin contact. That's what would do her some good.

"You should get some sleep," he said, his voice gentle and rumbling with restraint. Like always, he knew exactly what she was thinking. He thought it was a bad idea.

He was right.

But, damn it. Mission sex with some of the best sex she'd ever had. Or maybe it was just sex with Declan. She'd never crossed that line with anyone else.

He withdrew his touch and devoured another bite of the casserole. He didn't meet her eyes as he said, "Go ahead. I'll clean up."

Was he...backing down?

Declan Reid?

"If I didn't know better, I'd think you were trying to get rid of me."

His fork stopped midway to his mouth, but he still didn't look at her. "We'll need to be sharp come morning. We find Tommy, we go home."

Again, no hesitation, no doubt. In his mind, they had a mission, and they would complete it.

"I can take the hint." She slid her chair back and stood. "But you're giving out mixed signals, and I've had enough therapy to know it's because you're covering. One minute, you're flirting with me, the next, you're pushing me away. Why?"

"Because I want what you aren't willing to give, and I keep hoping you'll change your mind. That you'll realize how much you mean to me and let me be there for you.

But, right here, right now?" He finally met her eyes. "You're struggling to keep it together, and you've just come down from the adrenaline high. You're exhausted and not thinking straight. I'm not going to take advantage of that."

She placed her hands on the table and leaned toward him, nearly nose to now. "Maybe I want you to."

"Why, so you can hate me again in the light of day?"

That remark hit too close to home. Was that what she was doing? Putting him in a no-win situation so she had a fresh reason to be angry at him again?

She straightened and rubbed a hand over her face. "I'm going to bed."

She lay down on the mattress, staring up at the ceiling. Sleep felt impossible. Everything was smothering her again, and she didn't know how to let it go. She willed her racing mind to quiet, but everything was tangled together, a web of emotions and responsibility that she couldn't seem to escape.

Declan slipped into the room on his way to the bathroom, and she turned on her side. He shut the door behind him before flicking on the bathroom light.

He was a beast in the field, but he was always considerate. Another thing she admired. So many men in his position lost their ability for compassion and simple, decent manners in their unwavering pursuit of duty.

Closing her eyes, she forced herself to take a deep breath. *Go to sleep*, she ordered herself. Dawn would bring more challenges, more questions, and she needed to be ready.

When she heard the shower come on, her imagination drifted to Dec's chiseled body, covered by the tattoos he'd acquired—one for every successful mission. Did he have any new ones?

Great, now she had a new reason for not being able to sleep.

Her body craved his.

Memories of their time together played in her head like a movie reel. Undercover ops, the adrenaline, the sheer high it gave her. The after-mission weekends in places around the world.

Her nipples were hard, the spot between her legs aching. It had been over a year since the last time he'd stripped her bare. Pushed her against the wall, pinned her under him, let her ride him...

But it felt so much longer.

The devil on her shoulder egged her on. She flipped back the covers, too hot now. Her core pulsed, desperate for relief. Her fingers ached to touch him, stroke him. Her tongue wanted to taste his muscles, her mouth wanted to gorge on his hard, thick shaft.

She slipped out of bed before she could find any more arguments to the contrary.

In the bathroom, she removed the T-shirt and sweatpants. He poked his head around the shower curtain, his eyes going wide. "What are you doing?"

"I thought you might need someone to wash your back."

She climbed in, running her fingers over his wet skin.

He froze, except for a certain body part that came to full attention.

She slid her hand over it, sighing at the familiar feel of it. *Yes, this is what I need.*

"Just sex," she said against his skin. "Okay?"

He started to speak, stopped as she stroked him. "Just sex," he croaked.

And then he grabbed her, hiked her up by her ass cheeks, and pinned her against the shower stall.

SIXTEEN

Their coupling was quick and dirty, hard and fast. Not exactly how Declan intended their reunion to go, but he'd take it.

Just sex, she'd said, but they both knew better.

There was no going back to that point in their relationship. They'd come too far, survived too much, for it to ever be different.

He carried her to the bed, his legs shaking with his spent pleasure, but when she bit his lower lip, he was already growing hard again.

She grabbed him to her, desperate fingers scratched at his shoulders, his back. His wild thing.

Her legs were still around his waist as they tumbled to the mattress, tangled in each other's limbs. Their mouths clashed in a hungry, claiming kiss.

He knew what she needed, and he intended to give it to her.

He pinned her wrists to the bed and tore his mouth

away from hers. He bowed over her, staring her in the eyes for a long moment, assessing her.

She squirmed under him. "Stop looking at me like I'm a mission. You don't have to figure me out."

But he did. It was how he worked.

He looked at every problem in order to find a solution.

He examined every option in order to find the best one.

He analyzed every move, optimizing for the outcome he wanted.

Right now, he wanted her screaming his name.

Giving her a feral grin, he kissed his way down her collarbone and lower. He_ flicked his tongue over one of her nipples. She arched and whimpered, so he sucked it into his mouth, grazing the sensitive flesh with his teeth.

She again made that noise in her throat, and his cock bobbed in response. Every time he got her under him, he told himself to take it slow. He wanted to savor her taste, suck and touch every inch of her. Once she was there, however, it took every ounce of his willpower not to rush.

"Every time I see you, I want you even more," he muttered against her skin, wet from his ministrations.

She tried to break free from his iron grip, but he held firm, sliding his tongue to her other breast and giving it equal attention. Licking, sucking, nipping it with his teeth.

"Declan," she breathed, a plea.

He loosed one wrist, skimming his fingers over her

flat belly and lower. Her knees fell open even wider, inviting him to touch her.

Releasing her other wrist, he knelt between her legs, propping her feet on the bed. She reached for him, trying to grab his shoulders, his neck, anything, but he batted her hands away. "Let me look at you."

Even in the dim light of the bedroom, he saw a pink shimmer on her cheeks. The tough, demanding side of Meg would never admit to it, but she was self-conscious about her body. About her delicious curves that he couldn't get enough of.

She arched again, impatient, and he lowered his mouth. She stopped moving.

He raised his focus to meet her eyes. Licked his lips.

She sucked in a breath of anticipation.

He kissed her first, a light, teasing press of his lips. He flicked his tongue across the bundle of nerves buried there.

"Oh...god..." she groaned.

He dragged his tongue through the swollen folds. She writhed.

He repeated the process. When she was panting, he filled her with his tongue, pulling out long enough to suck on her sensitive spot. Like he'd done with her nipples, he raked his teeth over it.

Swollen and wet, she was close to climax already, having never fully come down from the previous one. He gave her another slow lick and suck before he slid two fingers inside of her.

She arched, saying his name as if it were a command.

He liked that, so he repeated what he'd done. "Come for me, Meg."

Her climax broke so hard and fast, she cried out loud enough to wake the neighbors. With his fingers and tongue, he rode out the climax with her, milking it for everything it was worth.

In the aftermath, he pulled her close, soaking in the feel of her against his body. She fit like a glove, and he knew it was too much to wish for, but he wanted this. All of it. He wanted her on his team and in his bed.

Her breathing evened out, and he kept an arm around her, smug that he'd satisfied her so thoroughly she could finally sleep.

He dozed as well, and when he woke, it was to her fingers stroking the length of his cock. He caught her mouth, and she closed her palm around him, giving him a squeeze. He pumped into her hand, sinking his fingers into her hair and tugging her head back so he could look her in the eye. "I want the record to note that it might be just sex for you, but it's not for me."

Through lowered lashes, she met his gaze. "I know."

She shoved on his chest as she climbed on top of him. With eager confidence, she slid onto him, one teasing inch at a time.

Pulling back, she kissed him, her tongue scraping over his teeth. She broke from the kiss long enough to whisper, "Don't hold back. I won't break."

That was all the permission he needed. He flipped her onto her back and drove himself into her.

Restraint frayed, he gave himself over to the need inside him.

Even that first time, in the shower, there was a part of him that was afraid to push her too far, too fast.

Not now.

Her nails dug into his back, and she met his eyes, egging him on. His body strained, heat tearing down his spine as his hips flexed. He slid deeper, retreated, plunged again.

Just as they were in sync on every mission, they were in sync in the throes of passion. As he breathed in, she breathed out. In and out. Their breaths, his cock. Her hips met every thrust. Her nails dug into his back.

In and out. In and out.

He took her mouth again, letting her breath fill his lungs as he thrust home again. She contracted around him, letting him stretch her. She took all of him inside her and wanted more.

Her hands went to his ass. He withdrew and slammed back into her, the force of it propelling her up the bed. She arched, and he lifted her hips, feeling her walls close around him.

This time, he gave her a final push, and she again screamed his name as she climaxed.

He pounded into her, his own following her over the edge.

Her walls tightened over and over again, ringing him dry. When they were finally both spent, he collapsed on top of her, but only for a moment. He started to take his weight off of her so he didn't crush her, but she gripped him tightly, refusing to let him move.

As it had during sex, their individual breathings seemed to line up as she kept him right where he was above her. She kissed the tight cords of his neck, squeezed her legs around his waist.

When he looked into her eyes, she ran a finger over his jaw. "It's more than sex for me, too."

He caught her lips and teased her tongue with his. "Good," was all he said before he shifted to his side, taking her with him and tucking her into his body.

SEVENTEEN

Dec brought her coffee and a couple of frozen waffles he'd toasted and served it all in bed.

The previous few hours had been a mix of sleeping and sex, yet something so much more.

She'd awakened to his hands and lips on her body, and instead of her first thought being about Jessie, it had been about him. The horrible memories had been held at bay for hours, allowing her to sleep without nightmares.

As they ate propped against the pillows, her hand snaked inside his briefs, and oops, wouldn't you know it, she'd smeared syrup on a particular part of his anatomy.

And well, she was then indebted to lick it off.

Which set off another round of lovemaking. This one broke the bed. One of the legs cracked, and the head-board ended up splintered.

"Tessa is going to be pissed," Meg muttered as Dec drew her into the shower.

Smiling like the satisfied and cocky male he was, he

fisted his hand in her hair and eased her head back, exposing her neck so he could kiss it. "Actually, I think she'll be pleased you finally embraced your wild child again."

Fifteen minutes later, she marveled at the welcome ache between her legs and the new memories she had. The old ones were still there, but the new ones were fresh and made her feel alive again.

She decided to focus on them. To focus on Dec and the sounds he made when she raked her fingers and then her lips over the new tattoos he had on various parts of his body.

When they finally came back to earth, he hustled her toward the back door, tossing her jacket at her. "We're meeting the taxi driver at the spot he picked up Tommy in twenty."

She shoved her feet into her shoes. "That's four kilometers from here. How are we going to get there in twenty minutes?"

"I thought we'd run. "

Her mouth dropped open. "You want me to run four kilos in twenty minutes?"

"Out of shape, recruit?"

He'd been a drill sergeant for part of his Marine career.

"I haven't kept up with my normal exercise routine, so sue me. I had other things to handle, and I didn't expect to be back in the field."

He dropped one of his big arms around her shoulders

and walked her toward the door. "Guess I'll have to carry you."

She was still griping at him when they rounded the corner of the house to find Tessa at the curb, waiting for them. The fall day was cool, but she had the windows of her car down, a techno dance beat filtering out as she motioned at them to hurry.

"I'm going to be late," she complaincd, putting the car in gear before Meg even finished closing her door.

"There's no way the taxi cab owner will willingly give us the information we need," Dec said. Inside the tiny car, he dominated the space. "I used the app to book the exact same taxi for a ride instead. Hopefully, it's the driver from yesterday—they typically drive the same routes—and we can question him."

Smart. "Beauty and brains," Meg teased, pinching his waist. "No wonder Flynn recommended you for the swans."

Tessa watched them in the rearview as she headed for the boulevard. She caught Meg's eye, understanding in her too-clever gaze.

Meg felt her cheeks heat. Shit. She was acting like her old self, which gave her away. The old Meg had been in love with Dec from the moment he'd challenged her on that first mission. Tessa hadn't been with them then, but Jessie had probably told her. Jessie and Tessa, thick as thieves.

The embassy was still a disaster in the aftermath, with barricades and yards of bright police tape cordoning off the block and parking lot behind it. Tessa tsked as she got them as close as possible, not far from the bus stop. "My beautiful building." She caught their eyes again in her mirror. "They're looking for you, you know."

"Who is?" Meg demanded.

"The media reported that two suspicious Americans were spotted roaming the embassy during the riots, and the Romanian police want them for questioning." She pivoted in her seat. "They don't have pictures of you, but they're circulating sketches. Pretty bad ones, but you should still be careful. I'm hoping my SWAT buddy doesn't point a finger at me."

"And Hagar? Are they saying anything about him?" Dec asked.

She shook her head. "I thought there would be a video of him and his death squad being arrested, but there's nothing."

The three of them exchanged a look.

"What's Flynn saying?" Tessa asked.

Meg's phone had a dozen texts and missed calls from him and Del. Among them was one from Spence, letting her know he had delivered the USB to their boss. That was the only one she responded to with a thumbs-up emoji.

The taxi arrived, saving her from replying. "Thanks for the ride, Tessa."

She and Dec bailed, Tessa calling out the open window, "Just keep me out of it, okay?"

That seemed to be the running theme when the two of them climbed into the back of the driver's car. "Where to?" the man asked in a heavily accented English.

Meg flashed her phone, Tommy's employment picture on the screen. "Do you remember picking up this man here yesterday?"

The driver barely glanced at the photo. "Nah." he pressed a button on the machine connected to his dashboard. "Destination?"

"Take another look," Dec ordered. "This is your route, right? You were here yesterday?"

Something about his tone caught the man's attention. He peered in his rearview at them, then reluctantly inspected the picture more closely. "Maybe."

The way Tommy had looked yesterday was a far cry from his clean-cut, smiling face in the photo. "He's American," she told the guy. "You picked him up after the bomb went off here. Surely, you didn't have that many calls for this place after that."

"All we need is to know where you dropped him off," Dec added.

"The meter is running. Do you want to go anywhere or not?"

Dec pulled out several bills and slid them through the wire bars between the seats. "Take us to the place you took him."

The man's eyes grew greedy as he took in the bills, but he said, "I prefer crypto."

"Or I could break your nose," Del countered.

"Get out," the man said.

Dec yanked out his phone. "Fine. Tell us what we want to know, and I'll pay with Bitcoin."

Frustration simmered beneath her skin. This was all

part of the game, and she knew it. She'd done this dance many times with other assets and resources. But right now, staring at the remains of the embassy and thinking back to yesterday, her nerves sparked with dread all over again.

"Maybe I don't want anything to do with this," the driver said. "Whatever this is. You should get out."

A greedy man with a conscience. It happened frequently when trying to bribe decent people. She could use that to her advantage. "His name is Tommy, and he's my brother," she said. It wasn't a complete lie. "He's in trouble, and I'm trying to get him out of it before he ends up dead. I know you picked him up here. I need to find him. Please."

The driver's gaze flicked between the cash and her face as he weighed his options. The war in his eyes told her he truly was a decent guy, but like most folks, barely paying his bills and keeping his head above water.

With a sigh, he snatched the money from Dec's hand, crypto forgotten and not above taking a bribe. That, combined with Meg's story, seemed to be the perfect formula. "I dropped him at the train station."

Train station. Damn. Tommy could be hundreds of miles away by now. "Did he say where he was going?" she asked.

The man tucked the bribe into his jacket pocket. "No. He was a quiet one, moody. Just told me to drop him there, and he didn't even give me a tip."

Dec slid him another bill. "Take us to the station, and

I'll provide you with a day's worth of pay—in crypto, if that's what you want."

The car grumbled to life, and he tapped in the destination in his machine. Now, he was all smiles and good manners. "You like music? I play you some."

Dec nodded, slipping his phone away. "What's your favorite?"

"Hip-hop," the driver said, making a U-turn and heading for the boulevard. "I like rap, too. You like rap?"

"Sure," Dec said. "Turn it up loud."

Meg winced as the driver did so, shooting Dec a *what the hell* look.

He drew her close, acting like her lover, as he muttered in her ear. "Where would Tommy go?"

Technically, Dec *was* her lover, so it wasn't hard to pretend she enjoyed the feel of his warm breath against her cheek. She shifted so she could speak into his ear easily as well, smiling in case their audience was watching. "Before Afghanistan, he did a six-week stint at the Berlin office. Berlin is familiar. He might go there."

Dec ran his fingers down her neck, across her collarbone, and her breath hitched. "If he's been stationed here, this would be more familiar, but after what happened, I assume he's left town. You know him better than I do, though. What do you think?"

She chuckled, arching her neck slightly and raking her fingers through his hair, keeping up the pretense. "I'm not sure what to think. I need to talk to Flynn about why Tommy was stationed here in the first place."

He grazed his lips over her exposed skin just under

her ear. Her thighs clenched. "I already did," he admitted.

She pulled back, dropping the act. "You did what?"

He put a hand on the back of her head and pulled her close again, kissing her. Teasing her lips apart with his tongue.

By the time he broke the kiss, they were both breathing hard. "We're fired, by the way," he murmured into her ear. "He did tell me that Tommy had been stationed here for the past six months. He put in for an open position and got it without any issue. Flynn says he's been working at getting back in the field ever since Jessie's death, applying for every job that came his way. Flynn made steered him here, thinking it was the best way to utilize his skills without putting too much stress on him."

That Dec had gone behind her back and talked to Flynn annoyed her, yet, having that information might help. "And what does Flynn think now that his golden boy might be a traitor?"

"He doesn't want to believe it any more than you or I do, but he's pissed. He's been Tommy's guardian angel since all this happened, and this is how the kid repays him?" He shook his head. "He gave me quite a lecture about us going off task, but secretly, I think he's rooting for us to find him."

She rested a hand on Dec's shoulder, brushed her cheek against his. "We all feel responsible for him."

He skimmed the bottom of one heavy breast with a thumb before sliding a possessive hand to her waist. His lips found that sensitive spot under her ear again, his teeth nibbling at it. "What is your honest opinion? Has he gone dark side, or is he working some elaborate plan to take revenge on Hagar?"

God, she was having trouble concentrating. She swallowed hard, the ache between her legs growing needy. "He's making it look like the former, but I'm hoping it's the latter."

He already knew that, but it was all she could get out. She kissed him then, not caring about the audience or their act. It wasn't an act anymore. Not for her.

Her second responded, and she knew from the way his lips took hers that it wasn't an act for him anymore, either.

The rap singer ended that song and began another. She quit caring about anything but Dec and his hands, his mouth, the looks he was giving her.

His eyes simmered with need and a greediness that had nothing to do with Tommy and everything to do with getting her clothes off. He planned to ravage her again as soon as he had the chance.

She was nearly orgasmic when they reached the station, and her legs trembled as she started to exit the car. Their driver was more than happy when Dec followed through with his promise, and they exchanged the information necessary for the man to receive his payment for a day's worth of work.

"Do you want me to wait?" he asked, almost hopeful.

"No, but thanks," Dec said, slapping the back of the

seat and quickly adjusting his pants, where a tell-tale bulge showed. "We appreciate your help."

"Name's Tomas." When Meg met his eyes at the name, he nodded. It was another reason he'd helped them. "I hope you find your brother. You need more help, you text me."

She thanked him and got out.

Inside the bustling station, they moved through the terminal, flashing Tommy's photo to the staff and security guards. At first, she'd been worried they might be recognized from the sketches Tessa had told them about, but no one seemed to pay much attention to them.

Meg's hope for a lead dwindled with each shake of the head, each indifferent shrug. No one had seen Tommy.

Had he even bought a ticket? Had he stopped here for some other reason?

Declan shared her frustration. "None of the clerks remember him, and if he did grab a ticket, he must have used an alias. If he didn't buy one, where did he go? Did he grab another taxi and head off somewhere else?"

While her partner appeared perfectly composed and calm, she could hear the strain in his voice. He preferred dealing with bombs and staring down the barrels of guns. Detective work wasn't his thing.

In all honesty, she preferred the adrenaline rush of action, as well. "If he thought someone was following him, he might have."

Dec glanced around at the crisscrossing patterns of travelers, at the giant clock and the boards listing the incoming and outgoing trains. "We need Del or Spence to check tickets, security camera footage, and other ride services. There's no point in taking off for Berlin unless we're sure that's where he went."

"Can we play on Flynn's guardian angel complex to allow one or both of them to help us?"

He steered her toward the nearest exit. "Guess we're going to find out. Once we're back at the safe house, I'll contact Langley."

But outside, they saw Tomas hailing them from across the street.

"What's he still doing here?" Meg asked.

"Bankrupting me?" Declan replied.

Once they could weave through the slow-moving traffic dropping off and picking up passengers, they met him at his car. At least they'd have a way back to the safe house.

They'd have to make him drop them off a few blocks away, but it would save a long walk or another call to beg Tessa for a favor. How many did Meg owe her now? She's lost count. "You're still here," she said to him. "Couldn't get any new customers?"

He glanced around nervously, lowering his voice. "Someone wants me to bring you to an address on the south side of the city."

Her heart skipped a beat. Dec moved a step closer to the man. "Who does?"

The driver shrugged, showing them his phone. "Unknown number."

They read the text that was brief and gave nothing away:

Bring the Americans to the following address. A token of my appreciation will be deposited into your money account. Do not disappoint me, or your family will pay for your negligence.

It was followed with an address. That was it.

"They made the deposit already," Tomas said, shifting his weight from foot to foot. "He didn't need to threaten my family. Is that what your brother does? Threatens innocent people?"

"How do you know it's from him?" Dec asked.

"Who else would it be from?"

Meg glanced at Dec. The threat didn't sound like Tommy, but then, he wasn't acting like himself. It wasn't much of a lead, but it was the only one they had.

He nodded in agreement.

Always in sync. She loved that about them.

He opened the door, and she slid into the backseat." No one's going to hurt your family. Just drive."

EIGHTEEN

The address was that of an abandoned mall—a sprawling, decaying husk of what it had once been.

Faded signs, shattered windows, and graffiti-covered walls greeted them as Tomas pulled into an empty parking lot.

The sky had darkened on the way, and rain began to patter against the windows.

"Drive around," Declan instructed. There were too many entrances, too many places for Tommy or whoever had sent that message to hide.

Too many places that could be traps.

"Just let us out here," Meg countered.

Even after the events of the previous day, Declan felt reluctant to lead Meg into the place without any backup or assistance. Yet, she was chomping at the bit to bail from the car and stride right in.

The woman was going to give him a stroke.

Normally, he was right beside her when it came to leading the charge, but for a brief moment, he considered hog-tying her and making the driver take her back to the bus stop. "We don't know what we're getting into," he argued. "We need to do surveillance."

Surprisingly, she didn't argue. "This is a huge place. Our host could be anywhere."

There were several broken-down, abandoned cars in various lots as Tomas eased around the gigantic structure. Grass and weeds pushed through the cracks in the asphalt. The once well-manicured trees and bushes in the islands were growing wild.

In what was considered the rear, Declan noted plain employee entrances that led to the individual shops. "Stop here."

His instincts were on high alert, and he palmed his weapon as he and Meg left their nervous driver with instructions to wait. The first door was locked, and so were the next several.

Rain dampened his clothes. The taxi continued to track their progress as they made their way down the long line of back doors. Eventually, Declan hailed the driver and told him to leave.

"Should I call the police?" Tomas asked.

"No. We'll handle it." Declan tapped the open window ledge, glancing up as the rain began to fall in earnest. "It's best if you go. We'll call you if we need anything else."

"Maybe we should have him stay," Meg said, watching the car slowly drive away.

In the distance, they could hear plenty of traffic on the roads, but here, only the sound of the car engine and their footsteps met his ears. Declan tried the next handle, another sign that read Employees Only denoted it as having once been a popular clothing store. "I don't know who's waiting for us inside, and I don't want another hostage situation."

She didn't argue or disagree. Step by step, they made their way around loading docks and more entrances that weren't for the public. Every single one was locked.

His hair was plastered to his head. Hers, too. He saw droplets caught in her long lashes and wished he could wipe them away. What had happened in the back of that taxi...

He had to tap down the memory or end up hard all over again. "Why do I feel like we're being herded toward the front?"

She wiggled the next metal knob and shook her head, using her shoulder to dry her cheek. What were the odds that all of these less obvious entrances were barred to them? "Because we are?"

The place was laid out like a wheel with four spokes. While the main entrance was the biggest and had a showy arched gateway, the others simply funneled shoppers into the stores, anchoring each spoke. "Looks like we're going to have to take our chances with a more obvious entrance," he admitted.

"I'll take lead."

Of course, she would. She always did. It ate at him—her need to be in charge. To prove herself.

"I know what you're thinking," she said. "But if it's Tommy, he'll be more likely to talk to me."

True. If he saw Declan coming, he might run again. "I'll hang back so I don't spook him, but if it's not him..."

"Who else could it be?"

As she stepped through the cracked glass doors into a shadowy lobby of what had been a department store, he followed a few steps behind. She peeled off to the right, and he did as well but kept his eyes and his gun fixed on the left. Blinking his eyes to adjust to the dim light filtering in from a mass of upper-story windows, he scanned what he could see. Most of those windows were also broken out, the squall dumping water inside. It drowned out the sound of their footsteps in the empty space.

No one jumped out from behind any displays or counters. Much like the embassy, this place looked like it had been overrun by people bent on destroying it at some point. A few items of clothing were scattered around, but most were ripped or trampled.

The place smelled of rusting metal, plastic, rotting food, and sweaty bodies. There were remnants of squatters and druggies. An escalator in the center of the anchor store had been torn up, and more graffiti decorated it.

They continued their counterclockwise path, encountering more destruction and remnants of the people who had used the place for shelter or other activities.

Eventually, they arrived at the exit into the main area of the mall. The light was dimmer, and they could hear the storm outside picking up, rain hammering on the roof high above their heads.

They moved as one, in and out of the smaller shops along the way, stepping over the refuse and wreckage that was everywhere but finding no inhabitants.

Declan thought that was good, and yet, it made this whole thing feel even more off than it already did. If Tommy wanted to talk to them, why go to such elaborate means to bring them here? Was he being followed? Had he put himself in so much danger that one of Hagar's allies or minions was tracking him?

Or was he afraid that Flynn was?

They passed a food court and arrived at what used to be the mall's central fountain. Declan was scanning the area behind them, making sure no one snuck up on them, when he heard Meg suck in a breath.

He pivoted at the sound, ready to fire his weapon, then froze.

Meg's voice came out strangled. "Tessa?"

The Architect was bound and gagged, slumped against the cracked stone of the fountain. One of her eyes was swollen shut, and the other swung toward them.

Meg moved, ready to run to her, but Declan shot out an arm to stop her. "Wait."

She froze, seeing the figures emerging from the shadows. Armed men moved with precision to surround the fountain's base and Tessa.

Bringing up the rear, swaggering to stand in front of her, was Hagar.

A machete hung from his hand.

"That's not possible," Meg stammered under her breath.

"A black swan," Dec muttered. Another surprise.

He felt rage rip through Meg. She raised her voice and shouted, "How did you escape?"

Declan's guts crawled as Hagar's eyes roved over her body. The things he wanted to do to her shone in them. "You must know by now that I am all-powerful."

"Meaning you have the Romanian Police in your back pocket," Declan clarified. "Plenty of assholes bribe officials. You're not unique or clever."

They were outnumbered and cornered. Tessa was his hostage this time, but it was all too similar to what happened with Jessie.

Declan would not let it happen again.

Meg started to speak, but her voice trembled. She cleared her throat, her back going ramrod straight. "What do you want?"

Hagar's cold smile stretched across his face as he took a single step forward. The tiniest bit of light caught on the blade. "Come now, my sweet Meg. You know what I want."

Declan stepped in front of her, a shield.

She stepped out from behind him. "Me," she said so softly, it was barely a whisper.

Hagar's smile grew. "We have unfinished business, do we not?"

"Fuck you," Declan said. "The only unfinished business is for me to put you down like the rabid dog you are."

Tessa shook her head, her eyes going to a spot behind Hagar on the fountain. Declan had missed it before, and now the sight of it made his skin crawl.

A second machete.

Meg laid her weapon on the floor, raising her hands. "Me for her," she said, gesturing at Tessa. "A more than fair trade."

Her voice was now without any emotion. Dead. Just like she knew she would be if she traded places with Tessa.

"Meg," Declan ground out.

"It's okay," she said quietly. "Take Tessa out of here. Don't look back."

She took a step toward Hagar, and it was all Declan could do not to tackle her. "All due respect, no," he said. "I said it before, and I'll say it again. I will always—"

"Release her," she interrupted him, speaking to the terrorist. "Let her go free, and you can have me."

The bastard licked his lips. He fucking *licked his lips*.

Declan brought his gun up and pointed it at the bastard's smug face, stepping up to where Meg's gun lay. *I will kill him. Before this day is done, I will use one of his own machetes and give him a dose of his own medicine.*

"Say it," Meg demanded. "I want your word that Tessa and Declan walk out of here, free and clear, if I give myself to you."

As if there were any honor to this man. As if she could trust anything he promised.

Hagar sized Declan up and glanced back at Tessa.

"Seems to me you don't have a choice in the matter. You are mine, regardless if I let them go."

Damn it. Declan had walked her right into this trap.

It was up to him to get her out.

She had some warped sense of righteousness that letting Hagar kill her would... What?

It wouldn't bring Jessie back.

It wouldn't absolve her from what had happened.

Did she still believe she deserved this? Deserved to die?

Bullshit.

Five of Hagar's death squad, plus Hagar himself. The odds weren't good, but Declan wasn't going down without a fight. He needed Meg to snap out of her guilt-driven sense of duty and help him out.

"Remember Winnipeg?" he said.

She blinked and turned her head ever so slightly, frowning. "Winnipeg?"

He stepped into her line of sight and gave her a wicked grin. "Yes, Winnipeg."

Her brows scrunched. "You can't be serious."

Hagar, no longer in the spotlight, took a bold step toward them. "What are you talking about?"

With a nod, Declan tossed Meg his gun. She caught it at the same time he grabbed her by the back of her dad's jacket and lifted her clean off her feet. "This, you motherfucker."

She screamed, partly in surprise, the sound morphing into a warrior's yell. As it was meant to do, it startled their target, even as Declan sent her flying.

Bam, bam, bam, she fired the gun as she sailed through the air, taking out two of the death squad before she crashed into Hagar.

They landed in a heap on the wet tile floor.

Tessa cowered but kicked out at the nearest goon when he fired at Declan.

Declan ducked and ran, swiping up Meg's weapon and slamming his booted foot into Hagar's head. He dropped to his knees, sliding across the floor and firing at the men still standing with both his and her weapons.

Meg unleashed another scream, but a bullet lodged in his arm, and he dove for cover beside the fountain. Somehow, Tessa managed to get to the machete and leverage it to cut the gray tape binding her wrists.

Declan leaped up on the rim of the fountain and struck the last squad member in the gut with a round-house kick. Toppling backward, the man sent a volley of bullets skyward and fell hard on top of one of his comrades. Declan jumped down and kicked the M4 away from the asshole's hands before he sent him to his maker.

From off to his right, another gun went off and another man fell, sightless, to the floor. Declan whirled to find Tessa holding the weapon she'd removed from one of the already dead men. The death squad were all dead.

Together, they turned to Meg and Hagar.

Declan froze. Hagar had his arm around her neck and held her in front of him, using her as a shield as he walked her backward one slow step at a time.

She staggered, a wound in her abdomen pouring blood. Blood dripped from the side of her lips, too.

In Hagar's hand, he raised his machete. "Put down your weapons, or she dies," he growled.

He wasn't without injury: blood trickled down his cheek from a gash at his temple. His nose was busted, and the blood that dripped from it coated his lips and teeth.

Declan stepped behind Tessa and shoved Meg's gun into the waistband of his pants, sliding out from behind her to lay his Sig down. Tessa let the M4 clatter to the ground.

Hagar shoved Meg to her knees in front of him. "You stole her from me," he said to Declan, "but she's always been mine."

Fuck, fuck, fuck. "Meg," Declan demanded, trying to get her attention. "Look at me."

Her eyes were distant, unseeing as she stared at the floor where her blood seeped across the tiles. Slowly, too slowly, they slid to him. "It's okay," she said again. "I remember Winnipeg and Serbia and all of them. Serbia is one of my favorites. Find Tommy for me."

Serbia? The goatfuck that...

Had he heard her right?

Hagar laughed. "You'll never find him. He owes me a great debt." He raised the blade. "Just like you."

Time expanded and warped.

Declan's heart stopped.

His chest locked up as the blade began to fall.

Serbia.

He reached for his waistband and winked at Meg.

You and me, he mouthed.

You and me, she mouthed back.

"Now," Declan yelled, jerking out her gun.

Meg offered him a ghost of a smile.

She fell to her belly. Rolled.

Tessa screamed.

Declan pulled the trigger.

NINETEEN

Her side hurt like a bitch. Meg stared up at the towering roof filled with broken and jagged skylights above her. The echoes of gunfire still rang in her ears.

Rushing footsteps, Declan's voice, Tessa crying...it all filtered through her ringing ears, seeming distant and fading.

Dec's face appeared above her. He sunk to his knees and ran gentle hands over her, assessing her injuries. "You're going to be fine," he said, even though he pulled up short when he touched her left side.

She coughed up blood. "Hagar?"

Men and women in dark clothes and caring weapons rushed the scene. Director Flynn appeared beside Dec, his face grim as he stared down at her. "Declan followed orders for once and didn't kill him. After that snafu with the Romanian police, I decided to step in and take over. Hagar has earned himself a one-way ticket to one of my favorite prisons."

A black site where he would be tortured and interrogated. Good.

A medic with a severe expression and carrying a duffel with a first aid cross on the end eased down on the other side of Meg. She assessed her in one quick glance, unzipped the bag, and shoved something from it at Declan. "Press this against the wound." She glanced up at the Director. "She needs a hospital before she bleeds out."

Flynn moved away, barking orders. The medic set up an IV and poked Meg in the arm with the needle. "I'll be all right," Meg assured Declan, even though she felt herself floating away.

He patted her cheek. "You're brilliant, you know that, right?"

She tried to smile, but her muscles didn't want to respond. Her body trembled, and her teeth chattered. "I'm cold," she whispered. "Really cold."

Then Spence was there, grabbing hold of her hand and squeezing. "You're going into shock. We're going to take care of you."

"Why are you...here?" she forced out.

Come to think of it, why was Flynn?

"Flynn and Del were in Spain, and after they found out I had the USB, they came here. Del has been working on decrypting the security on that drive. I've been tracking your phones." He gave her hand another hard squeeze. "As soon as we found out Hagar had been released and you guys were at the train station, Flynn decided it was time to step in. He claims he came here to fire you, but I think he wants to insert himself in our hunt for Tommy." He gave her a wink.

The medic handed the IV bag to Spence. "Hold this up and keep it above her head." She called to somebody over her shoulder. "We need to move her."

The room was growing dim. Meg blinked at the dozens of black spots blurring her vision. "Is Tessa...?"

Declan shushed her as the medic gave her a shot of something. "Enough talk for now. You need to conserve your strength."

"I'm fine," Tessa's voice called from across the expanse.

"Sanitize the place of our presence," Flynn ordered those with him. "Blindfold Hagar, and let's get out of here."

Someone handed Declan a blanket, and he wrapped it around her. "This is going to hurt," he said. "I'll make it up to you, I promise."

And then he lifted her from the floor. She wished she had something to bite down on, but she didn't. A scream tore from her throat before everything went black.

THREE WEEKS *later*
   The Farm

MEG THOUGHT she was going to die.
   In fact, she wished she would.

Death would be a step up from the torture Dec was putting her through on the obstacle course from hell.

He'd already made her run two miles. A slow, grueling two miles since she was still recuperating from the damage Hagar's machete had done to her.

But, by God, she was up and moving. Her internal organs were on the mend—sore but restored to functionality after emergency surgery and a second follow-up. The puckered skin was still pink, but the stitches were dissolving, and she had found a tiny bit of appreciation for it since Dec had been massaging the area with oil every night before they went to bed.

"Keep crawling, Carson," he barked, his clipboard and stopwatch in hand. "You're losing time."

Sweat poured down her face, and she was completely covered in mud, her body aching from trying to get back into shape. She hated every minute of it but knew she needed it. Her muscles remembered all of this, and yet, in only three weeks, she had lost most of her strength and endurance. She had completed several rounds of physical therapy. It wasn't enough.

The Farm. Declan. Those were the things she needed.

When she wasn't training physically, Flynn had her sitting in a cubicle analyzing Hagar, his allies, and the information that Del had so far retrieved from the USB. When no one was looking, she ran searches looking for Tommy. It wasn't the same as being in the field, but at least she felt like she was doing something.

Flynn knew, of course. He kept tabs on every

keystroke and every phone call she made, but he didn't reprimand her. They all wanted to find him.

As she crawled through the mud, every breath she took was for Jessica. For the Black Swans. For her. She was going to be a team player again, even though Flynn refused to discuss putting her back in the field. She was too much of a wildcard, he said, and she didn't deserve to lead the swans anymore.

He was full of shit, and she was going to prove it to him. She'd told him so, in fact.

"I look forward to it," he'd replied like the bastard he was. "Show me what you've got."

Declan's muddy boots were in sight as she dug her elbows into the mud and grunted. "Come on, Carson. What is this, your day off? Acting like a girl again, are you? Thinking I'm going to cut you some slack?"

Once a marine, always a marine. Once a drill sergeant, always a pain in her ass.

She didn't have the energy to flip him off, but later... Oh, yeah, later, he would pay for those insults.

She made it to the finish line and collapsed at his feet, barely able to hold her head out of the mud. She heard the click of the stopwatch and his pen scribbling on his clipboard. "Thirty seconds slower than yesterday. Tomorrow, you better pick up the pace."

He didn't give her any quarter, which was exactly how she wanted it. She would rebuild her body, her mind, and her relationships. Tawny and her family were at the top of that list. Declan, Tessa, and Spence were too.

She would learn to depend on others and not try to do everything alone.

That would be harder than repairing the damage to her body, but she would do it.

"Can you handle a couple of rounds in the boxing ring this afternoon?" Dec asked.

She rolled over onto her back, staring up at his face, framed by the blue sky above. All this physical activity cleared her mind and brought her clarity she hadn't had in months. "I'd like to visit Jessica's grave instead."

He offered her a hand. "Would you like company? "

Typically, she would've dismissed his help and gotten to her feet by herself. Today, she slipped her hand into his and bit back a groan as he pulled her up. She didn't need his help, but she needed to get used to allowing it. "I think I'd like to go by myself."

He nodded.

Across the way, Spence appeared, waving a hand at them. "Flynn wants us in his office in thirty."

Her heart jumped. She looked at Dec. "Tommy," she whispered and moved as fast as her aching body could for the showers.

TWENTY

Conrad Flynn paced behind his desk as Reid, Carson, and Sterling filed in. They took seats positioned on the other side, sharing glances between them.

"You were there," Meg said. "Platja Fonda."

He'd wondered when she'd piece it together. "Julia insisted we take a vacation. She likes the beach, and we'd never been there. Pretty spot, but too full of tourists for me."

She didn't buy it, giving him a flat stare. She had yet to put back on the weight she'd lost after Mendoza's death, and he sometimes caught her grimacing when she moved wrong, but the heavy shadows were gone from under her eyes. She'd regained much of her confidence.

"Why didn't you make yourself known to me?" she asked. "Hand me my orders in person?"

Because he preferred to keep his balls intact. "We both know the answer to that. If I'd shown my face, you would have considered it an act of aggression. It would've ended badly for both of us."

Reid snorted. As always, he was grizzled and stalwart —loyal to his team and his country. 'Rugged' was the term Julia used when talking about him.

Flynn thought dangerous was more accurate.

He was a cunning one, as well. He could run circles around most of the operatives in the field these days, and Conrad appreciated that. There was no hiding behind technology, analytics, or theories with Reid. He was a boots-on-the-ground, take-no-prisoners kind of guy.

But Meg Carson? She was her own brand of weapon of mass destruction these days. She had no regard for her own safety and seemed determined to throw herself on her sword to make up for what had happened to her teammate.

There was no making up for that. It was a heavy loss, and Conrad understood the guilt and regret she lived with every hour of every day. If he could've taken it away from her and dealt with it himself, he would have. He had his own demons that he fought on a regular basis, people he hadn't been able to save, but no amount of self-flagellating could bring Jessica back.

All they could do was move on.

"Mosai Hagar was found dead inside his prison cell last night," he said.

Carson's mouth dropped open.

Reid and Sterling didn't so much as blink.

Good men.

"How?" Meg asked.

Conrad observed her, noting how her gaze started to slide to her right, where Declan sat stone-faced. It snapped back to him.

"A silent assassin, apparently," he told her. He wanted to say, "A ghost did it" but that would have given too much away. "No one was caught on the security feeds. We have no leads, and I, for one, don't give a shit if we ever do."

He'd wanted to do it himself, but it wasn't his kill. If he'd thought Meg could have handled it, he would have allowed her to do it. As it was, he made sure he, Reid, and Sterling had gone to that black site deep in the Virginia mountains last night and returned before morning.

"Are you okay with that?" Conrad asked.

Meg seemed speechless, then nodded. "Guess I have to be."

He punched a button on his phone, hailing his secretary. "Get Contessa Vulpe on the line for me."

"Yes, sir," Kate responded.

"Tessa?" Meg asked. "What's this about?"

Conrad sank into his chair, picking up a pen and tapping it on his blotter. "Del and Spence have broken through another layer of encryption on Tommy's drive. I've also recovered intel from Tommy's superior—against his boss' directives, he'd been digging into an investment firm in Russia and following a money trail he believed backed up his suspicions about Hagar's involvement in a potential black swan scenario."

Declan and Meg looked at Spence, who cleared his

throat and sat forward in his chair. Conrad gave him a nod to go ahead and explain what they had found. "Our boy uncovered a plot to set off multiple EMP bombs at US military bases across the globe," Spence told them. "Plenty of conspiracy theories about such a thing have existed for a while, and the Department of Defense has taken measures to ensure that never happens, but this..." He shook his head as if still trying to wrap his mind around it. "It goes all the way back to the businesses supplying the superconductors for the military's computers."

Such weapons had been around for a while, the US being one of the countries at the forefront of designing non-nuclear tools in order to destroy information systems. They'd created devices small enough to fit in a briefcase, making them not only feasible but also practical.

Kate's voice interrupted. "Contessa Vulpe line one, sir."

"Thank you." Conrad punched the button. "Tessa, you're on speaker. The swans are here, and we're discussing what Tommy uncovered and put on that USB." He brought her up to speed and then continued, "As you know, EMPs can cripple electronic wiring and circuitry over several square miles, posing a threat to infrastructure. The Defense Department's reliance on satellites and commercial computer equipment to command military forces and operations worldwide is threatened. Much has been done to take precautions to offset such attacks. Still, if what Tommy uncovered involves sabotage of the superconductors used in military computers, all of these bases are sitting ducks. Our nation's infrastructure, as well. Forces we have around the world, the same. It could be a nightmare."

Tessa's voice came through the speaker. "Is that why Hagar wanted the drive? To destroy the evidence?"

"Yes. We believe he was to play a part in the dispersion of the e-bombs, and because of his showmanship in murdering Jessica in front of the world, he put a glaring spotlight on himself. Those in charge of the bomb attacks, whoever they are, didn't like that in the least."

Spence rubbed his palms on his slacks. "Tommy probably tripped a red flag while digging into that Russian investment company. The leader of the e-bomb attacks realized Hagar was no longer an asset to their master plan, but the plan was already in play. The best they could do was to try and destroy any evidence Tommy had."

"And kill him, along with it," Declan added.

Meg rubbed a hand over her face. "Oh, Tommy. Why didn't he come to us with this?"

Conrad didn't want to remind her that she'd been off the grid since Jessica's funeral. "It's not surprising that he has trust issues or is seeking retribution for what happened to his sister. He did speak to his supervisor about his concerns, but unfortunately, Marchetti isn't an operative. He's an ambassador. His job is to keep the peace, not stir the pot. After speaking with him, it's my understanding that he thought Tommy was obsessed with Hagar and that any intel he provided about the man was skewed. Tommy was, after all, stationed there as an actual

State Department employee, not a CIA agent. He and Marchetti butted heads frequently over his job duties."

"How long before we find out what else is on that USB?" Declan asked.

"Tommy developed a personal encryption program," Spence said. "It's quite impressive. Could be a while."

Meg frowned. "Do we have a lead on him?"

Conrad tapped his pen impatiently. "He's still in the wind, either by choice or because he's been kidnapped by one of Hagar's former allies." Meg had suspected the same thing based on the research she'd been doing. He saw the way her face tightened at his confirmation of her fears. "Our search for him continues."

"You're putting us back in the field," Declan said.

He didn't want to. Meg wasn't ready. They were still one member short of a full team.

"Tessa," Meg said, reading his mind. "Our fourth."

He nodded.

Tessa said, "I don't think that's a good idea."

Meg shifted to the edge of her seat, leaning toward the phone. "We worked well together in Bucharest."

"I don't do spy shit anymore, remember?"

Meg started to reply, but Conrad waved a hand at her. "I'm not asking you to do spy *shit*," he said. "I'm putting you on the team to find Tommy."

Meg bristled, straightening her back and giving him the hairy eyeball. "While it's my team, and I get to say who's on it," she clarified, "we would welcome your skills, Tessa."

She didn't yet realize it wasn't her team anymore.

"First of all,"—he tapped his pen—"you're in no condition to be in the field, and also, I fired you. Secondly, your team exists because of me. You report to *me*. I get the final say about who's part of the Black Swan Division and who the leader is."

Reid and Sterling tensed. Meg came out of her seat, planting her hands on his desk. "You're kicking me off the swans? You can't do that. It's *my* concept. My idea to create this team. I'm its leader."

It was the least he expected from her, and it was good to see her fired up again. Not that dead, hollow woman she'd been. But...he wanted her to work for it. "The USB was a test to see if you could handle being in the field again. You failed."

She shot straight up, opened her mouth, slammed it shut.

Reid spoke up. "That's not exactly true. We did recover the USB, sir."

"And then disobeyed orders," Conrad reminded him.

Meg glanced at her second, then turned shocked eyes on Conrad. "You're kicking Dec off the team, too?"

He tossed the pen on the blotter and rocked back in his chair. "Unless the two of you can convince me otherwise, yes. Why should I allow you to stay part of this division and go after Tommy?"

Meg's hands went to her hips, and Conrad settled in for the presentation she was about to give.

BUCHAREST

. . .

IT WASN'T EVEN 5 PM, but because of the storms that had been moving through the city, Tessa had to turn on lights as she listened to the argument on the other end of the phone. She wanted to hang up on them, but all she did was hit the mute button as she stared out the third-floor window of her loft.

This area of the city was busy with the end-of-day traffic that would only grow worse over the next few hours as people headed home from their jobs. Her view was only of another high-rise across the street, but she loved it anyway.

This section had once been a garment district, the businesses going bankrupt in the early 2000s and falling into disrepair for years until real estate investors came along and snatched them up. Each of the buildings had been completely overhauled, turning them into apartments and revitalizing the three-block radius into a hub of niche stores and short- and long-term rentals that attracted a younger crowd.

Her split lip had healed, and only the last remnants of her black eye were apparent. Those she covered with makeup when she went out. She'd had to use some of her vacation time initially so she didn't have to answer awkward questions at work about her appearance, but she wasn't into vacations anyway.

A knock sounded at her door, and she frowned. She wasn't expecting company—hell, she never expected company.

Taking the phone with her, she checked her security camera and saw nothing—whoever was out there was staying out of sight.

She glanced through the peephole in the door, and as she did so, her visitor slid into view. She nearly dropped the phone.

She threw back the three locks on the door and yanked it open.

In the past year, Tommy Mendoza had put on muscle. His hair was longer than she remembered. He looked older than his thirty years, but those eyes... They were the same soulful brown as his sister's.

"Tessa?" Meg's voice came from the speaker. "Are you still there?"

"What are you doing here?" she asked Tommy, keeping her voice low even though her end was muted. "Are you all right? "

He glanced up and down the hall before meeting her eyes again. So haunted, so damaged. "Can I come in?"

A big debate raged inside her but damn it. She couldn't turn him away.

She ushered him across the threshold, closing and locking the door behind him.

"We've all been looking for you," she said.

"I know." He scanned the loft, taking in the brick walls the investors had left for ambiance. The high ceilings that showed the duct worked. The neutral colors she preferred with a splash of brightness in the pillows and rugs. His gaze locked on a picture on her fireplace mantle. It was of her and Jessica at The Farm on the day Jessie had passed her final test.

Tessa hadn't had a best friend since grade school. It was just how she was—she didn't let herself get close to anyone. Bad things happened when she did.

She let herself get close to Jessie, and look what had happened to her.

She swallowed the lump of emotions that rose unbidden. "I was closer to her than my own sister," she confessed.

He touched the frame with reverence. "She felt the same about you, you know?" He glanced at her, his hand falling to his side. She knew that look. It was the one you got when you'd been on the run for a while. When people were after you, trying to kill you. He needed a shower, a shave, and fresh clothes. Twelve straight hours of sleep and a few decent meals. "I need your help."

"Tessa?" Meg called again. "Can you hear me?"

Everything inside Tessa reached for the kid. He was only seven years her junior, and yet, she thought of him as such.

And even though she should think of him as a brother, she couldn't. Those eyes, that brain...

Few men had captivated her the way he had from the first time she'd met him. She'd never acted on her feelings for him out of respect for Jessie, but now...

She punched the mute button. "I need to call you back," she told the swans and Conrad Flynn.

She disconnected and tossed the phone on the coffee table, motioning for Tommy to sit on the couch.

"You look good, T," he said.

For a second, she couldn't move. Couldn't think. They'd always shortened each other's names as a joke. 'TNT,' Jessie had called them. 'Two sticks of dynamite.'

Explosive. What she was about to do might take her down a dark and dangerous path. She cleared her throat and affected an outwardly calm face. "And you look like you could use a drink."

He hesitated before removing his jacket. While he laid it on the arm of the sofa and sat, she admired how he filled out the gray shirt underneath. The way his jeans hugged his hips. "Better make it coffee. I have a long night ahead of me."

Turning away so he couldn't see her smile, she headed for the coffee maker behind the kitchen island. Her pulse hammered, her breath coming too fast. "Coffee it is."

Because if Tommy was here, it looked like she was in for a long night, too.

WANT MORE of Declan and Meg? Read their Origin Story, an exclusive in my subscription membership Thrill Rides!

Join Thrill Rides here: https://mistyevansbooks.com/membership-levels

Read The Prague Mission here: https://mistyevansbooks.com/the-prague-mission-declan-meg-origin-story-exclusive

Read Meg and Dec's interview here: https://mistye vansbooks.com/meg_dec_interview

MEG AND DECLAN are okay for now, but Tessa's in danger. Don't miss her story in Tempting Tessa, releasing March 2025!

Turn the page for more!

DON'T MISS TEMPTING TESSA!

She's chasing the truth; he's chasing her—but neither can outrun their pasts.

WHEN YOU'RE BETRAYED by the very people you swore to protect, trust is the deadliest weapon of all.

Former CIA operative Tessa Vulpe has left the spy life behind—until she's forced back into the highly classified Black Swan Division to help track down missing State Department employee Tommy Mendoza.

Tommy went dark while hunting the killer behind his sister's death, only to resurface on Tessa's doorstep.

As they work to uncover a twisted network of conspiracies, a betrayal from within Black Swan threatens not only their mission but their lives.

In a world where loyalty is a luxury, surviving demands the ultimate sacrifice—of trust, of duty, and maybe even of each other. With danger closing in and the line between betrayal and loyalty blurring, Tessa and Tommy must face the truth: the dead don't always stay buried, and the past never forgets.

Perfect for fans of fast-paced espionage thrillers, Tempting Tessa weaves high-stakes action with an unforgettable romance against a backdrop of betrayal and redemption.

PREORDER NOW!

And be sure to sign up for my newsletter so you're the first to know about new releases and giveaways.
I want Misty's Newsletter!

VISIT MISTY'S STORE

Did you know you can buy directly from me? When you do, the retailer doesn't take a cut and I can pass on the savings to YOU!

https://mistyevansbooks.com/shop

Benefits:

You can find ALL my books in one place

SAVE money

EARLY access to new releases

Special Collections, Boxed Sets, and Limited Editions

Support a small business (and support a dream!)

Why Buy Direct?

When you purchase a book by your favorite author, electronic or print, on retailer platforms, the company keeps 30-70% of the sale, leaving the author with little to no profit (after the company deducts delivery fees, taxes, and other fees).

Buying directly from the author means that more goes to them so they can keep turning out stories for you. Every published story, every book, requires cover art, editing, and hours and hours of the author's time simply to create it. Not to mention overhead costs, such as websites, newsletters, writing software, graphics programs, advertising, taxes, etc.

In addition, one of the big-name retailers requires exclusivity, and all of them have terms of service and rules and regulations that make it challenging and time-consuming for an indie author to navigate the publishing world.

Most of us would MUCH rather spend our time creating more stories for YOU, rather than trying to jump through the hoops at the retailers. Buying direct from your favorite authors (where available) helps ensure that an author you love is not subject to unexplained account closures, withholding of royalties, censorship, and other issues that can affect their livelihood.

I've experienced ALL of these. By buying direct, you help put control of my work back in my hands - and I can continue to write more.

Either way, thank you for supporting me! I under-stand buying direct doesn't work for everyone and even if you use the retailers to buy my books, I appreciate you!

Happy reading,

Misty

https://mistyevansbooks.com/shop

YOU'RE INVITED!

Do you have a passion for my stories?

Want more from my characters?

How about early access to ALL my new releases?

My reader community is for YOU!

Try my **Thrill Rides reader community** for a month! It's ONLY $2.99 - you're buying me a coffee - and in return, you get all these perks:

Writing Updates so you know what's in the works and how soon you can get it

Special Content, including chapters in new and upcoming stories

FREE Access to new books - Read all of my new suspense and thriller releases for FREE before they're available at retailers

Don't miss out on this opportunity! Join my Thrill Rides reader community today.

https://mistyevansbooks.com/membership-levels

**Don't want to miss a single release? Join my
newsletter!**

Black Swan Division Romantic Thriller Series

Redeeming Meg

Tempting Tessa

Avenging Jessie

SEALs of Shadow Force Series

Fatal Truth

Fatal Honor

Fatal Courage

Fatal Love

Fatal Vision

Fatal Thrill

Risk

SEALS of Shadow Force Series: Spy Division

Man Hunt

Man Killer

Man Down

Covert Affairs

Covert Tactics

Covert Obsession

The SCVC Taskforce Series

Deadly Pursuit

Deadly Deception

Deadly Force

Deadly Intent

Deadly Affair, A SCVC Taskforce novella

Deadly Attraction

Deadly Secrets

Deadly Holiday, A SCVC Taskforce novella

Deadly Target

Deadly Rescue

Deadly Bounty

Deadly Betrayal

Deadly Threat

The Super Agent Series

Operation Sheba

Operation Paris

Operation Proof of Life

Operation Lost Princess

Operation Ambush

Operation Contraband

Operation Sleeping With the Enemy

Operation Heist

The Justice Team Series (with Adrienne Giordano)

Stealing Justice

Cheating Justice

Holiday Justice

Exposing Justice

Undercover Justice

Protecting Justice

Missing Justice

Defending Justice

SCHOCK SISTERS MYSTERY SERIES w/Adrienne Giordano

1st Shock

2nd Strike

3rd Tango

The Secret Ingredient Culinary Mystery Series

The Secret Ingredient, A Culinary Romantic Mystery with Bonus Recipes

The Secret Life of Cranberry Sauce, A Secret Ingredient Holiday Novella

PNR & UF BY MISTY/NYX HALLIWELL

The Accidental Reaper Series

Grim & Bare It, Book 1

Reaper's Keepers, Book 2

In too Reap, Book 3

Killin' It (short story for newsletter subscribers only)

The Vampire's Kiss (an exclusive short story available in Misty's Store. *Intended for mature audiences 17+*)

Grave Girl

Grave Magic

Grim Vows

The Kali Sweet Series

Revenge Is Sweet, Kali Sweet Series, Book 1

Sweet Chaos, Kali Sweet Series, Book 2

Sweet Soldier, Kali Sweet Series, Book 3

Sweet Curse, Kali Sweet Series, Book 4

Witches Anonymous Step 1

Cozy Mysteries (writing as Nyx Halliwell)

Sister Witches Of Raven Falls Mystery Series

Confessions of a Closet Medium Series

Hearts & Haunts

Vows & Vengeance

Cupcakes & Corpses

Tea Leaves & Troubled Spirits

Haunted Honeymoon

Wedding Bells & Psychic Spells

Phantoms Are Forever

Sister Witches of Story Cove Series

Cinder

Belle

Snow

Ruby

Zelle

Sister Witches of Story Cove Complete Set

***

Witchy Candy Shop Mysteries

Tricks and Treats

Candy and Creeps

Gum and Ghouls (releasing 2025)

MEET MISTY & NOLAN

USA TODAY Bestselling Author Misty Evans has published over ninety novels, as well as nonfiction inspirational journals. She loves writing urban fantasy, paranormal romance, and mystery/suspense. Under her pen name, Nyx Halliwell, she also writes supernatural cozy mysteries.

When not reading or writing, she enjoys music, movies, and hanging out with her husband, twin sons, and three spoiled rescue dogs. She's a crafter at heart and has far too many projects to finish.

Visit www.mistyevansbooks.com to check out her online store and sign up for her newsletter.

Misty's son, Nolan Evans, has been a lifelong reader and has taken the plunge into writing. When not crafting stories for the Black Swan Division series around his day job, he enjoys music, hiking, traveling, and spending time with his cat, Winnie.

LETTER FROM MISTY

Thank you for reading this story! It is an honor and a privilege to write books for you. I'm an indie author and every fan is important to me. I pour my heart into each story and do my best to bring you an escape from the real world.

Readers are the key to my success - not a traditional publishing deal (had four), an agent (had two), or a publicity team (yep, you guessed it, had several of those as well.)

Those of you who read my books, love my characters and worlds, and then tell others about them are the best of friends. I adore you and will keep writing if you keep reading!

If you'd like to learn about my other books, sales, and special promotions, please sign up for my newsletter at **www.mistyevansbooks.com**.

You'll FREE stories, whether you love my suspense or my paranormal.

Support me directly (no retailer taking their cut), grab special edition box sets, and get new releases before they are out at retailers by visiting my store **https://mistyevansbooks.com/shop**.

I have sales and offer NEW RELEASES early (and at reduced prices)! Check it out.

Last but not least, if you enjoy clean, cozy mysteries, visit my pen name **www.nyxhalliwell.com** to see those books.

Thank you, and happy reading!

Misty